THE SECRET TAJ

Joanna Hamilton arrives in Delhi to accompany Mandy Robbins, the winner of a competition run by the *Daily Post*, on her prize of a tour of Northern India. Chaperoning the bored and rebellious teenager is no easy task, especially when the trip is being filmed for a TV documentary and the director is a demanding and autocratic genius called Matthew Howard. Despite all her misgivings, Joanna finds herself falling in love with him, but her dream is shattered when she is told that her love could ruin his brilliant career. Even the serenely beautiful Taj Mahal has a role in their tempestuous love which grows amid the colour and squalor of the real India.

THE SECRET TAJ

Stella Whitelaw

CHIVERS LARGE PRINT
BATH

British Library Cataloguing in Publication Data available

This Large Print edition published by Chivers Press, Bath, 1995.

Published by arrangement with the author.

U.K. Hardcover ISBN 0 7451 2916 1
U.K. Softcover ISBN 0 7451 2925 0

Photoset, printed and bound in Great Britain by
Redwood Books, Trowbridge, Wiltshire

THE SECRET TAJ

CHAPTER ONE

As the Boeing 747 taxied along the runway, its silver body shimmering in the heat, Joanna's heart quickened. They had arrived in India, that scorched and dusty country, and her first foreign assignment was about to begin.

She had already discovered on the long flight from London that escorting Mandy Robbins, the Magic Carpet girl, on her prize winning trip to Northern India, was not going to be easy. But even though Joanna was apprehensive about the task ahead, she could not suppress a tremor of excitement as she caught the first close glimpses of the Indian landscape.

As the steward pushed open the door of the air conditioned cabin, searing gusts of heat blew in from the red-earthed plain.

Slight and graceful in her flowing jade patterned sari, the air hostess stopped by Joanna and put her slender hands together in the old custom of namaskar.

'Namaste, Miss Hamilton,' she said in her lilting voice. 'Welcome to India.'

'India ... where anything could happen,' Joanna smiled to herself.

She blamed the birth of this great adventure on the print unions of Fleet Street and the circulation war which now gripped all the national daily newspapers. Some bright spark

1

on the *Daily Post* had thought up this Magic Carpet competition and the prize was not a simple package tour for two, but a cultural investigation of the old and modern India in Agra and Delhi. The trump card was that a television company had shown an interest in making a documentary of the tour, and the winner of the competition had every opportunity of becoming a television personality.

Even the flight had been unreal, enclosed in the first class cabin of the big jet, confused by the shifting hours of darkness. It had been impossible to sleep, although the in-flight film had passed a few restless hours.

Chasing the rose-streaked dawn, they ate hot croissants for breakfast high over the red plains. They flew from Karachi to Bombay, these brief stops giving them tantalising glimpses of the country they were going to travel.

Joanna looked across the aisle to the reason for their journey. The Magic Carpet girl, Mandy Robbins, gazed out of the cabin window with avid eyes, her fingers groping in her huge bag for the vast collection of make-up without which it seemed no teenager ever moved ten yards. She began to repaint the smudged black lines round her eyes, their expression a mixture of sulkiness and glory. This trip was going to be the making of Mandy Robbins, and nothing was going to stop her.

2

She saw fame stretching ahead of her like a golden stairway.

'The sign has gone off. You can unfasten your safety belt,' said Joanna.

'I can read,' said Mandy. 'You don't have to treat me like a child.'

'Good,' said Joanna, trying to sound cheerful. 'Then I can rely on you not to behave like one.'

What a choice prize winner Joanna had been landed with ... there had been something wrong every mile of the flight. The pillow too hard, the blanket itchy, there was not enough leg room, her chicken was tough, the magazine old, she had seen the film before ... Mandy had complained about everything, and seemed to expect Joanna to do something about it.

'I feel sick,' said Mandy.

'I expect it's just the descent after that rather large breakfast,' said Joanna, remembering the way Mandy had helped herself to all the extras. 'There's no hurry. We can wait a few minutes until everyone else has got off. Well, I won't be needing a coat any more, that's for certain. I can feel the heat from here.'

She leaned over to help Mandy unfasten her belt. 'Come on, Mandy,' she said encouragingly. 'There'll be a film crew waiting to take shots of your arrival. Then we'll book in at our hotel and you can have a shower. You'll feel better then.'

'My legs have gone all funny,' said Mandy,

3

not moving.

'Nerves,' said Joanna patiently. 'Take some deep breaths. If you don't hurry up, we'll still be on the plane for its return flight to Heathrow.'

The pert little face swung round to meet Joanna, the short blonde curls bouncing, baby blue eyes wide and innocent.

'Don't you hurry-up me, Joanna,' she said. 'We'll go when I'm ready.'

Joanna swallowed any retort which she might have made. She was here to cover the tour for the *Daily Post*, however difficult. It was still a matter of some amazement to Joanna that she was in India at all, for Nancy Rees Owen, their clever and talented columnist, had been earmarked for the story. She had caught mumps from her youngest child, and that was how Joanna, only ten weeks on the *Post*, found herself in Mr Wilberforce's office, having first class air tickets thrust into her hand.

'Me? Why me?' she had gasped.

'Because we can't spare anyone else,' he said candidly. 'We've got too many big stories blowing up. Heavens, this is a piece of cake. There's nothing here you can't handle. I want lots of the feminist point of view, the girl's reaction to India, lyrical stuff about India ... I bet you wrote poetry when you were a kid?'

'Well, er ... yes,' Joanna admitted.

'Then you're just the person. Don't let the

4

film crew browbeat you. Your work is just as important. Just watch out for Matthew Howard, the director, and don't tread on his toes. He's an arrogant bastard and he'll want everything his way. I'm relying on you to remind him that the Magic Carpet girl is the *Daily Post*'s property and your responsibility.'

'Yes, Mr Wilberforce, I'll try,' said Joanna, trying to sound enthusiastic. Of course the idea of going to India was fun, but she was still so new on Fleet Street. If she failed then her chance of another job would be bleak.

'Right, that's settled then. You'd better go and get your jabs. We don't want you going down with yellow fever.' It was meant to be a joke, but Arthur Wilberforce was desperately disappointed that Nancy Rees Owen was not covering the trip. This slim young woman with chestnut brown hair was an unknown quantity. 'Good luck,' he added, holding out his hand. If she fouled it up, he could easily replace her. He knew it was not fair.

'Remember, no scandals,' he said, waving her out of the office.

'I won't let her get pregnant, if that's what you mean,' said Joanna.

Joanna had been frantically busy those last few days. No one gave her any time off for shopping, and she found herself packing the same old summer dresses that had been hanging about, unworn, for several years. Mandy was to be the fashion plate in her

5

£1,000 worth of donated designer clothes. Joanna had only to look neat and tidy and very professional. She had decided that the only way to deal with Matthew Howard was to treat him as an equal, cool and determined, and not to be cowed by his fame and fortune.

She had taken time to look him up in the cuttings library. There was quite a file on Matthew Howard. He had shot to fame with a spectacularly stunning space film called *Planet Eleven*. He had written it, directed it, masterminded a lot of the outstanding visual effects, and now he could sit back and let the money pour into his bank account from every corner of the world. He need never work again. Joanna wondered why he was in the least bit interested in making a documentary for television about India.

His face looked out from the grey page of a newspaper, the photographer having caught a gleam of sardonic amusement in half closed eyes as the flash blinded him. It was a fudgy picture but the dark brows were drawn together, and the angular jaw had a hint of cruelty.

There were very few pictures of Matthew Howard. It seemed he did not like being photographed, or seen in public. There were few personal details about him. It was obvious that reporters were not exactly his favourite people.

Joanna began to collect up Mandy's

belongings on the plane which were strewn everywhere. She felt momentarily sorry for the girl. Mandy was a very young, if spoilt, seventeen year old, and newspapers could be monsters. They did gobble people up for the sake of their readers. But no one had forced Mandy to enter the competition.

'You'd better put a comb through your hair,' Joanna suggested. 'There'll be some photographers as well.'

Mandy made a reluctant show of teasing her curls. She hated being told anything. She looked at Joanna scornfully; no one would be taking her photograph. She thought her plain and pale and no competition whatsoever; even that chestnut hair was so unfashionably smooth and straight. And she was too tall for a woman. Men looked at small women with very high heels ... Mandy stretched out her legs, admiring the strappy sandals on her shapely feet.

'Good-bye. I hope you had a pleasant flight,' said the hostess standing in the doorway, the wind whipping the folds of her sari, hair escaping from its glossy plait.

Joanna shrank from the heat that came up in waves from the hot tarmac. It was like facing an open oven.

Mandy put her hand on the rail of the steps and took it away quickly with a cry. The metal was burning. The dark-skinned steward caught her arm as she almost fell.

'I've burnt my hand,' Mandy wailed. She glanced at Joanna to make sure she had heard. 'And I've left my camera behind. Will you get it?'

Joanna sighed and hurried back. No 'please'. I'm supposed to be a journalist, Joanna thought grimly, not a nursemaid. What could she write about Mandy's arrival at Delhi; the truth? That Mandy was feeling sick, had burnt her hand, and had managed to be rude to almost everyone she spoke to? Not exactly what Mr Wilberforce was expecting.

The steward helped Mandy down the steps and then escorted her to the white airport building. Joanna hurried to catch them up, the heels of her shoes sinking into the soft tarmac with every step.

They were met by officials from the airline, press and Embassy in the VIP arrivals lounge. Garlands of marigolds and jasmine were hung round their necks in greeting. Mandy was enjoying all the attention, her face flushed from the heat. Everyone was very helpful, easing them through the formalities. The lilting accent was strange and she had to strain to understand what was being said.

The noise was deafening. It seemed that for every passenger, there was a dozen or so voluble relations to meet him, or see him off. It was a kaleidoscope of colour with the women in gorgeous saris, some striped with silver or gold; flowers in their long glossy hair; the men in white shirts or tunics; the many coloured turbans.

Joanna kept the smile on her face and the conversation flowing. She was well practised at the art, while all the time keeping a look out for the film crew, and longing to kick her shoes off.

Mandy was hanging onto the arm of the air steward, who by this time was looking faintly embarrassed, although pleased and delighted.

'You'll have to let him go,' said Joanna in a low voice. 'He's not part of the prize, and you'll probably get him the sack.'

'I don't care,' said Mandy, shrugging her shoulders. 'I like him. He thinks I'm marvellous.'

Joanna gritted her teeth, and turned a half circle away. As she turned her glance went up to an open terrace above them. Leaning precariously over a rail with a shoulder camera was a member of the film crew. There was another man and a woman, and, quite recognisable at that distance by his height and distinctive bearing, Matthew Howard. He was looking down at their group with studied calculation as if they were creatures in a glass case.

Joanna felt a surge of anger. How dare he film them without their knowing? He had obviously seen Mandy's behaviour with the steward, and the little fracas between them just now. Joanna certainly was not going to have the tour spoilt at this stage by candid camera tactics.

'Don't move,' she said to Mandy so sharply that the girl looked at her in surprise. Joanna swiftly found the stairs to the upper floor and strode towards the film crew. It seemed to consist of only four people, three men and a woman.

As she approached the group, the tall man emerged briskly and almost walked into her.

'I'm just coming to see you,' she said.

'And I'm coming to see you,' he retorted. 'Get back downstairs. I haven't finished yet.'

That brief exchange took Joanna's next words away. She was used to being brushed aside, even to meeting rudeness, but this was more than plain bad manners. It was open hostility.

He flashed a glance at her, taking in the slimness of her hips in the navy skirt, the boyishness of her figure under the white silk shirt. His eyes raked her like an x-ray machine. He probably even knew that her shoes were too tight.

'So you're the Magic Carpet girl,' he drawled. 'You're wearing the wrong colours for your hair, and your posture's bad. I don't know why you tall girls always have to slouch.'

Joanna took a deep breath. The grey newspaper photo had not prepared her for the vividness of his blue eyes under those smouldering dark brows, nor the crispness of his thick black hair. He had the usual American male tan, and his whole body proclaimed a masculinity which Joanna found unnerving.

'Mr Matthew Howard?' Joanna said smoothly. 'I am indebted to you for the personal remarks. I must say your shirt is completely the right colour for your complexion, though it's a pity about the dandruff. My name is Joanna Hamilton, *Daily Post*, London. You will be aware that the winner of our Magic Carpet competition is a seventeen year old, Mandy Robbins. I am flattered by your mistake. I suggest we meet at the hotel to discuss your plans for filming, and my arrangements for the tour.'

She turned on her heel. She did not think she could continue the cool, determined stance for many moments longer. It had been quite a speech. His shirt was a muted plum and green tartan. There was no dandruff.

'And no more sneaky filming please,' she added defiantly. 'It isn't nice.'

He laughed, a short deep sound.

'I couldn't see the crows-feet from here,' he remarked.

Joanna went down the stairs quickly but carefully. This was no time to trip. Gradually her control returned and her natural sense of humour admitted that the exchange had its funny side, although Mr Howard had not been joking. She wondered if he ever took time off from being unpleasant.

Mandy was standing in the crowd, looking sullen and picking at the flowers in her garland.

'You left me a long time,' Mandy accused. The steward had gone back to his duties and she had felt abandoned. 'I'm tired of this. When are we going to the hotel?'

At last they were in a private car heading along the dusty road from the international airport to New Delhi. They were booked to stay at the Ashoka Hotel, one of the biggest hotels, but not the most modern. Joanna stared, fascinated, at the teeming traffic which crowded the bumpy, uneven road going into the capital city. There were swarms of cyclists, risking life and limb at every junction, bicycle rickshaws, horse-drawn tongas, motorcycle taxis, hand-pushed carts, and sacred cows plodding among the traffic. They wandered freely knowing that no one would harm them. They were sacred to the Hindus.

The streets were a mass of people; everyone seemed to be on the move, except the pedlars who had spread their wares on the pavements, and the shopkeepers sitting outside their open fronted shops.

Joanna had never seen so many people; poor villagers, beggars, well dressed merchants and civil servants, beautiful women in every colour of the rainbow, saris, punjabi tunics and trousers, gauzy scarves blowing in the hot wind ...

'It's so hot,' said Mandy, wiping her neck with a Marks and Spencer handkerchief.

Sun-bleached shrines and tombs lined the dry brown road to Delhi, their inscriptions faded, the wall paintings flaking but still bright despite the summers of many years. The ancient past mingled with banks of flowering shrubs and flowering trees along the road ... purple jacaranda, yellow laburnum, scarlet gul mohur, each filling the air with sweet heady fragrance. Joanna let the strange sights and sounds and smells wash over her. This was the India she had flown so far to see.

With a shriek of brakes, the car swerved into the drive leading to the Ashoka, a towering T-shaped hotel dominating acres of beautifully kept gardens.

The doorman, resplendent in a scarlet and gold uniform and spotless white turban, moved forward to open the car door with a flourish.

Mandy's spirits recovered as she saw the splendour of the hotel. This was more like it.

It was built on the lines of an Indian palace. Marble steps led to the revolving doors which opened into a lofty, pillared porchway. The splendid foyer was on two levels, each with thickly carpeted stairs taking them further into the hotel, a vast area which eventually widened out into a flower filled lounge as large as an ice rink. It was cool and quiet, despite the hum of

13

air conditioning, and the uniformed bell boys moved on silent feet. Beyond the panoramic windows were more gardens and flowering trees, rioting colour and leafy palms.

Huge erotic tapestries hung on the walls, mysterious and disturbing. Joanna had not expected such explicit scenes to be in a public place. The nubile statues of either sex were also sensual, their meaning clear, despite the exquisite draperies and exotic head-dresses. Yet the great room was as still and aloof as a cathedral, quite apart from the crude yet delicate art which decorated it.

Mandy caught sight of the arcade of boutiques with windows full of inviting clothes, brassware and brocades, saris and souvenirs. She had always wanted to stay in a really grand hotel. She could meet anyone here ... her fantasies soared as the lift took them to the sixth floor. The brown-eyed lift boy stared at Mandy all the way.

It's because she's so fair, thought Joanna, noticing the boy's inability to take his eyes off Mandy. Her big china blue eyes and curly blonde hair were such a complete contrast to Indian girls. No wonder he was staring.

Their luggage had already arrived at their suite. The adjoining rooms were large and cool, elegantly decorated and furnished in pale colours, each opening out onto a wide balcony. Each had a vast bathroom, marble tiled, with a deep bath big enough for two, and gold

14

dolphin shaped taps. A refrigerator stood in a corner, fully stocked.

'Don't forget it's against the law to drink alcohol in public in India,' said Joanna. 'There'll be iced mineral water in the fridge, so if I were you, I'd stick to that.'

'Well, you're not me, are you?' said Mandy, throwing herself down in a big armchair. 'I drink vodka and tonic at home.'

'Really? At your age?'

'I'm not a baby.'

'I'm aware of that,' said Joanna, determined not to get into a fight with Mandy. 'Now I've got lots of arrangements to see to, so I'll leave you to freshen up. I'll come and let you know what's first on the itinerary.'

Joanna paused in the doorway that led from the hall to her own room. She really did want the tour to go smoothly and Mandy to enjoy herself. Joanna could admire without envy the girl's youth and confidence, her femininity and air of helplessness. Men would always be opening doors for Mandy.

Mandy returned the gaze. She was almost contemptuous of the other woman, not wanting to admire the way she held down a difficult job in Fleet Street. Joanna's simple suit and casual hair style did not spell success to Mandy.

Joanna went into her bedroom and shut the door. The last hours had been exhausting, and she was tired from the long flight and lack of sleep. She longed to put her head down on that smooth, clean pillow and let herself drift. But there was so much to be done first.

She rang room service and ordered a tray of tea. At least Mr Wilberforce had allowed generous expenses for the trip. If she did not sit down and drink something, the nightmare would return ... she knew the warning signs. She knew the slight throbbing in her temple, the tingle in her fingertips, the strange heady feeling that overwork and exhaustion always brought on.

If she shut her eyes she would see Bruce and the waves of memory would flood through her mind and the nightmare begin. She began to take deep gulps of air, fighting the emotion down. It was not so often that she thought of him now, but when she did, the grief was as poignant as if it had all happened only yesterday ...

Their room service was fast and efficient, and a white-uniformed boy brought the tea on a silver tray. It was beautifully laid with the inevitable vase of small flowers and a dish of sweet rice cakes called idlis, and flat brown honey cakes.

Joanna made herself come back to the hotel room in New Delhi. So many people told her it was not healthy to dwell on the past, but it was not easy, even for a young woman. She had picked up the threads of living again, carved herself a career. Bruce would have been proud

16

of her.

Work had become her therapy. Long hours on a local newspaper covering council meetings, political rallies, the local carnival, writing up the weddings and obituaries, working herself to a standstill so that she fell exhausted into bed at night and slept. The work habit stayed with her as she progressed to a provincial evening paper, then a stint on a national news agency, and now, seven years later, she still filled her days with the same frantic pace. It was this reputation for hard work which landed her a staff job on the *Daily Post*.

Joanna asked the boy to take the tray out onto the balcony where a cushioned cane chair and a small bamboo table invited leisurely surveillance of the scenery. She would give herself fifteen minutes for tea, then she must start thinking about her first Magic Carpet story.

She closed her eyes as she sat back in the comfortable chair, the wind cooler at this height, the voices from the hotel pool far enough away to be just a pleasant background of laughter.

'Delhi laid on a floral welcome today for Mandy Robbins, our Magic Carpet girl as she drove from the airport to the grand Ashoka Hotel in New Delhi,' she composed mentally. 'This is the most wonderful day of my life,' said Mandy, clapping her hands with delight...'

17

Joanna groaned aloud. It was awful, absolutely pathetic, crumb journalism. This meaningless rubbish would not enhance her reputation or sell a single extra newspaper, except perhaps to Mandy's family. If only Mandy would say or do something original, react in some way ... any way.

Somehow she had to make Mandy bright and intelligent with an original slant on these new experiences. She wondered how Nancy Rees Owen would have coped.

Not a single creative thought came into Joanna's mind as she leaned back and munched a rice cake. The view was fascinating and revealing. The straight tree-lined avenues of New Delhi stretched right to the walls of the old city; the new government offices dominated the skyline while further in the shimmering horizon stood the dusky-red stone mosques and palaces of the Mogul Emperors. Nearer glimmered the shining blue domed minarets of the Pakistan Embassy appearing through a canopy of pale green leaves. The scent of a million flowers wafted to her balcony and chased away the last shreds of that headache with light fingers ... Joanna sighed with relief.

'Groans and sighs,' said a deep voice. 'I hope you are not going to be a noisy neighbour. I shall have to ask to have my room changed.'

Joanna did not turn her head. 'I was enjoying five minutes of peace and quiet.

Would you mind going away?'

'The *Post* are not paying you to idle about,' said Matthew Howard, leaning on the rail of his balcony. 'So if you don't mind we'll iron out our schedule problems now. I've no intention of spending the entire trip arguing with you about who is doing what when. Not that I ever argue with a woman. I always have my own way.'

The audacity of the man ... Joanna was about to come back with a stinging retort, when he leaped over the dividing concrete wall and arrived on her balcony. It was not that the wall was high, but it curved upwards to give maximum privacy to each occupant, and this slope was smooth and without footholds. Matthew Howard had taken the wall in one huge bound, quite careless of the fact that they were six floors up.

'Show-off,' said Joanna, shaken.

'Ah,' he said with mock disappointment. 'You've read that I was once a stunt man.'

'And the Olympics, of course,' she added scathingly.

'You know all my secrets. Well, since I'm here, I may as well have a cake,' he said, settling himself in the other chair. 'Aren't you going to offer me a cup of tea? Where are your manners?'

'No cup,' she said with saccharin sweetness. She had no intention of washing out her cup for him. 'Sorry.'

'I'll have it in the milk jug. I'm not fussy. We can ring down for some more milk if you are an excessive tea drinker. Yes, you look like a three cup person.'

'We could ring down for another cup,' said Joanna, icily.

'When you know me better,' he said, leaning forward and pouring himself a jug of tea. 'You will realise that when I want something, I want it immediately. I don't want to wait while they fetch a cup from some kitchens half a mile away. I want my tea now, hot and in a jug. Pass the sugar please.'

Her hand was almost shaking as she passed him the sugar bowl with its silver tongs. She did not know whether this was nerves or anger. Their glance met over the silver tongs. She knew that she ought to be laughing at this comical situation, but this man put her on the defensive.

The jug shrank to mug size as he cupped it in his strong, lean hands. She noticed the long, artistic fingers flexing round the heat from the china. He had an air of absolute authority, of superiority, of total confidence in what he was doing, and that whatever he did was right. That he had worked his way up to this position of influence and immense wealth was to his credit, but still the blood of princes flowed in his veins. It was the leanness of his jaw that held a hint of fine breeding, and the curl of a nostril; his colouring was of a Highlander, so was his

20

height. Was a great-grandparent the secret child of some Highland prince, stolen away in the night from the birth-bed of some raven-haired lassie? Joanna smiled to herself as her imagination took flight.

'Good heavens, the woman can smile. Does that mean I can have a honey cake?' he drawled.

Joanna held out the dish and he took two; this time she did not look at him, for every time she saw those dark Atlantic-blue eyes, she seemed to be at his mercy.

'Tell me,' she said casually. 'I'm curious. Why is it that the successful writer and director of *Planet Eleven* is bothering himself with a low budget documentary about a teenager touring India? It doesn't make sense.'

'It makes very good sense,' he said. 'I'm in the happy position of being able to do exactly what I like in this world, providing that I make the occasional commercial to pay the tax man.'

'*Planet Twelve*?' Joanna suggested.

'I think *Planet Eleven Point Five* would be more subtle. I've always wanted to film India but have been too lazy to do anything about it. Five hours a day by my pool in LA and even making a phone call is heavy work. So this television company approached me, on all fours, knowing they could never meet my price, but I liked the idea. I like my crew getting work and a regular wage. All I wanted was a free hand to do it my way, no interference and as many honey cakes as I can eat in a day.'

He was telling her quite politely that he would stand no arguments with her, and in any clash of opinion, she would lose.

'You'll get fat eating so many sweet things,' said Joanna, retreating to trivia.

He leaned forward suddenly, his hand reaching out to her shirt front. For one frozen moment, Joanna wondered what he was about to do. But he merely fastened a button, his fingers just brushing her soft skin.

'You can talk,' he said. 'You're popping out of your shirt. It's not fair to a hot-blooded man like myself, or was it on purpose?'

Joanna found the colour rising in her face, not just because of his audacious words, but because she could still feel the electric shock of his touch. She was embarrassed too because he would have seen her bra, a wisp of skin-coloured lace that barely covered her breasts, that was such a contrast to the plain skirt and tailored shirt.

'It was in preparation to having a shower, Mr Howard,' she said more calmly than she felt. 'Don't worry; you're not likely to be seduced by me. I could never fall in love with a man like you. I have very high ideals.'

'That is an immense relief, Miss Hamilton. I'm glad I am in no danger from you. Anyway, I prefer blondes. And talking of blondes, isn't that little Miss Shirley Temple herself down by the pool, surrounded by young men?'

Joanna peered below at the riot of colour. On the well-kept lawns strutted a pair of peacocks, their jewelled tails fanning the velvet grass. She caught sight of a slight figure in a scarlet swimsuit, her feet dangling in the pool, the sun glinting on golden curls.

Joanna shot to her feet with a cry of alarm. Matthew's fingers tightened on her wrist.

'Hang on,' he said. 'You're not her nursemaid.'

'You don't understand,' she said, wrenching her arm away. 'I'm responsible for her. It isn't easy.'

She glanced at Mandy's room as she ran barefoot through the small hallway. The door was open and garments from the prize wardrobe were scattered all over the floor.

Joanna ran along the corridor to the lift. She did not even know if the girl could swim, let alone take care of herself among a crowd of males. Mr Wilberforce was right. It was a big responsibility. She realised she had not even mentioned their schedules for the next day with Matthew. It would have to wait.

Outside the hotel she followed the gusts of laughter and sound of splashing.

It was packed around the pool, all nationalities, skins of all shades, pale pink, coffee, deepest brown. Joanna searched anxiously. She could not see Mandy anywhere.

Joanna gave a shiver despite the heat of the day. She was not concentrating. Those dark

23

fathomless eyes were unforgettable which annoyed her even more than her own edginess. She hoped he was not watching her from the balcony; she would not give him the satisfaction of looking up. She straightened her back.

'Mandy? Mandy...' she called out.

CHAPTER TWO

'Have you lost someone? Is there a reward?'

Joanna looked round to see who was speaking. A man was briskly towelling his wet fair hair until it stood out like porcupine quills. The handsome young face under the untidy hair was a startling contrast.

'You look real worried. Surely it can't be as bad as all that?' He had a slight foreign accent, difficult to place.

'I know it sounds quaintly Victorian but I have this girl in my care while she's away from home, and I simply can't have her disappearing every time I leave her for a few minutes,' Joanna explained in a rush. 'She's in a red swimsuit, fair curls, and quite pale because we have only just arrived.'

'Ah yes... I know who you mean. She is over there, under that green umbrella with half of the Embassy staff. Why not forget her? She's all right. Come and have a swim.'

Joanna felt over-dressed among all the bare backs and legs, all browning nicely under the hot Indian sun. There was nothing she would have liked more than to go swimming with this pleasant young man.

'I'm afraid you don't understand the situation,' she said wearily. 'I'm not being paid to go swimming...'

She caught sight of Mandy sitting at a table, tightly wedged in a group of laughing, bronzed young men. One of them had his arm lightly across the back of her chair. In front of her was an enormous mound of pink ice-cream sundae in a dish, and she was sucking an iced lime drink through two long straws. Her face was animated for once, blue eyes smiling up at the young man who had now moved his arm to casually stroking the back of her shoulders.

Joanna had a vision of herself fending off hordes of predatory men all the trip. The ice-cream and lime drink were probably made with water out of the tap and the girl would be ill tomorrow and that would be the end of any filming. And her copy for Mr Wilberforce ... she had not got a single idea for today yet.

'Hello, Mandy,' said Joanna. 'I didn't know where you were. I was worried.'

'This is the dragon I was telling you about,' Mandy announced, barely looking at Joanna. 'She guards me night and day.'

'You don't look like a dragon to me,' said the wet young man who had followed Joanna across to the table.

'I certainly am a dragon,' said Joanna crisply. 'And I'll guard Mandy night and day, if I get the chance. I can also spit fire if necessary.'

'Take cover, boys!'

Joanna saw Mandy's expression change as she caught a glimpse of the fair-haired young man standing behind her. He was handsome with incredibly curled eyelashes and dark Latin eyes. He smiled down at Mandy.

'Perhaps I should introduce myself,' he said. 'My name's Pierre Dupuis. I'm with Matthew Howard's film crew. I'm the sound man. I shall make you sound as pretty as you look, Miss Robbins.'

It was like the answer to a prayer. With one sentence the young man had melted Mandy's resistance to doing what she was told. Matthew Howard had made a clever choice with the young French Canadian. Had the other two, the cameraman and the woman, also dual roles?

'I think I'm starting to burn,' said Mandy. 'I go red ever so quickly.'

'Well, we don't want you with a face to match your swimsuit so we'd better buy you some protective cream right away.'

Mandy did not seem to care about the beautiful clothes she had been given, for the matching striped poncho was lying at her feet in a crumpled pile. Joanna picked it up and shook it out. It was like having a child to look after.

'I'd rather you didn't just disappear without telling me,' said Joanna as they went into the hotel. 'Please try to remember that I'm responsible for you.'

Mandy appeared not to be listening. Joanna sighed. She was going to need a lot of patience in the next few days. Reporting union meetings and break-ins in London was beginning to have a certain safe appeal; at least she knew what she was doing with routine stories.

They went to the hotel arcade to buy some cream for Mandy's skin. Matthew Howard was coming out of the most expensive dress shop, a black and gold box in his hands. One dark eyebrow lifted fractionally and Joanna realised that she was still barefooted. At least he could not accuse her of being stuffy.

He introduced himself to Mandy, and she was suddenly all flashing eyes and excited innocence. There was no trace of the sulky madam now.

'I really am thrilled to be working with you,' Mandy gushed. 'You're such a marvellous director. Everything you do is wonderful. This film about India and me will probably walk off with all the prizes at Cannes and just everywhere...'

Mandy could already see herself at Cannes, glitteringly dressed, on the arm of this famous film-maker, arriving for the award ceremony.

Joanna could barely conceal the disgust she felt. Nothing Mandy said or did gave her a line to write about. And now she was toadying up to Matthew Howard, and he was loving it. Or was he? That sardonic face really gave little away. Did he always dissect people as if they were nothing more than camera angles and lighting problems? No, she had the feeling that his perception of people went very deep, or he could not have made such a brilliant film as *Planet Eleven.*

She had seen the film twice because she realised that there were new and subtle nuances to discover in it with each viewing ... historical mysteries were hinted at, a lost character from a famous classical novel made a fleeting appearance, the clues for the future were there to be unravelled if one was observant enough.

Such a clever and inventive imagination made her feel a very ordinary hack journalist, but it still did not give him the right to be patronising. But Joanna was realistic in that aspect; he was a passing ship she had to cope with for the trip, and nothing more. She thought the simile of a ship was rather good. He was like a ship, ploughing relentlessly through everyone and everything as if they were nothing more than water.

He was talking to Mandy now about the filming, and she was listening with rapt concentration. It was the first time Mandy had shown any real interest in the arrangements.

'Tomorrow morning we are going to the zoo,' he was saying. 'All good little girls should have a day at the zoo. Then in the afternoon we will go to Rajghat and on to the Red Fort. A day of contrasts ... nature, death and the might of the Mogul Emperors ... as seen through Mandy's eyes.'

A glimmer of doubt appeared in her baby blue eyes. She did not really care for nature, death or emperors, but still this man was irresistible.

'I'll do whatever you say,' she said meekly.

'I don't want to be filming shadows under those pretty eyes,' he went on smoothly. 'So I suggest an early night. I'm sure you didn't get much sleep on the plane. Pierre will escort you to supper in the hotel and make sure you have everything you want.'

Mandy looked momentarily sulky at being sent to bed, then she cheered up at the mention of Pierre. She teetered off on her absurd shoes, wondering which of her new dresses to wear, and how to enslave that very handsome young man.

'Neat,' said Joanna. 'But that's my job. I'm supposed to be with her every waking moment, early suppers included.'

'Your job is to liaise with me about the filming schedules and the itinerary of this trip. You've done precious little yet.'

'That's hardly my fault,' Joanna snapped. 'I was coming to see you. I can't help it if Mandy likes wandering off.'

'We shall make a very early start,' said Matthew. 'The hot mid-day is not a good time to work, and early morning is the most pleasant part of the day. I'll take you out to dinner and we can continue this talk. We are going somewhere special, so wear this.' He thrust the black and gold box into her hands. 'Your clothes are all wrong.'

With this remark and a slight nod of the head, Matthew strode away across the vast foyer, his hands in his pockets, supreme male confidence in the set of his strong shoulders and slim hips.

Joanna felt like throwing the box in one of the ornamental ponds in the garden. The nerve of the man. To assume firstly that she would dine with him ... though she knew she would. That could count as work. But then to dictate what she should wear. She would definitely wear one of her own dresses, even though she had brought nothing new or special. Her clothes were all of good quality, simple and bought to last.

She stood in the shower letting the tepid water run over her body like a waterfall. She could have stood there, half dreaming, for hours but water was not plentiful and there were discreet notices about conserving water and switching off unused lights.

While she dried her hair, brushing it till the chestnut lights shone like streaks of autumn

30

sunshine, she concentrated on what she should write so far. Mr Wilberforce was expecting to run the series the moment he received the photographs. She had to confirm with Matthew Howard's cameraman that he would take a few extra shots for the newspaper.

She took an apple green shirtwaister dress from the wardrobe. Mr Howard could be offended. She put two tortoiseshell slides in her hair, a touch of lipstick, beige sandals and she was ready. She looked cool and neat.

The opulent black and gold box was still on the floor where she had left it. Her feminine curiosity overcame her and she could not resist lifting the lid. Swathes of tissue rustled as she lifted out the dress.

It was like something she had never seen in her life before ... yards of gossamer light as air, silk chiffon in a pale amber shot with hazy strands of gold, watery green and blue. It was like looking into the sun-streaked depths of a coral reef; as the material moved in her hands so the colours changed.

Hardly knowing what she was doing, Joanna stepped out of her shirtwaister and slipped the creation over her head. The soft chiffon fell over her body in whispers, her arms seeking the armholes among the mysterious folds. The dress was voluminous and yet so fine that it clung to her body and she could have crushed its width in one hand.

She looked in the mirror ... an amber vision

31

stared back, every pert contour of her figure revealed by the clinging material. The colour did something to her hair and her skin, making her hair more vibrant, her skin paler. She longed to wear it, to stun that so arrogant Mr Howard, to turn heads, to make a sensational entrance.

But she couldn't. The dress was an odd length, showing a few inches of slim ankle and the wrong shoes. She was about to take the dress off when she saw a pair of pale gold mesh mules in the box, and a matching slim purse. Drat the man; trust him to think of everything. As she stepped into the high heeled mules she knew that she would wear the outfit. No woman could resist it. But tomorrow she would return it, she decided firmly.

As she went along the wide corridor, the silk chiffon floating, heads did turn. The lift boy, who was daily surrounded by beautiful women, showed her out of the lift as if she was a princess.

Matthew Howard walked across, his eyes taking in every detail. He was wearing a white one-buttoned tuxedo, a pale blue shirt open at the neck, and darker blue slacks. It showed up his tan, those blue eyes and crisp black hair.

'Not bad,' he said, moving to view her from either side. 'Do you like it?'

Joanna longed to lie, but she could not. 'It's beautiful,' she said. Then reluctantly she added ... 'thank you.'

'Your face isn't right,' he said, taking the purse out of her hand. 'Let's see what you've got. Heavens, you travel light for a woman. I wish I had my make-up girl here to show you what to do. You've got nice shaped eyebrows but they need defining.'

He moved her over to a mirror and a brighter light, and took a pencil from her purse. Lightly he stroked her eyebrows, a few deft strokes that suddenly made her brows exist.

'Do you mind?' said Joanna, incensed. 'I will not have you doing things to my face in a public place.'

'Where do you want me to do it? Do you want to come up to my room?' he mocked.

'Excuse me, but that's my lipstick!'

'Lipstick, rouge, what does it matter?' He put some on the tip of his fourth finger. 'What does matter is that we do something about bringing out these delightful hollows ... there ... a little on those bones makes all the difference. Thank goodness, you've got mascara. I was beginning to think all was lost. Put some more on, girl, lashings of it. You've long lashes, make them longer. Don't be so half hearted about it.'

Joanna's hands were trembling as she found herself obeying his orders. The day must come when she could pay him back for this humiliation.

He was taking the slides out of her hair.

33

'Nice pins,' he commented.

'How kind of you to say so,' said Joanna, but the scorn was lost on him. 'They were my mother's.'

'I'm sure your mother would have agreed that this is the way to wear them.' He scooped her hair up and off her neck, securing the loops with the two slides. 'You need to take the bulk of your hair away from the face. Let's see your face. Don't hide it behind all that hair.' He began searching the carpet area in a curious manner, then came back to her. 'You can always find a hairpin on the floor when you want one, even in a luxury hotel.' He twisted the pin into the loose cluster on the top of her head, and stood back.

'Not bad,' he said again.

It was an amber goddess that Joanna saw reflected in the mirror, tall and svelte in shimmering colours, colt-like ankles, a tumble of hair on her head with stray tendrils on her cheeks and touching the back of her neck; and her face ... she almost did not recognise the sudden haughty bones and wild colour, the smoky eyes rimmed with dark lashes. A smile came to her mouth as she thought of Shirley Maclaine in *Sweet Charity* singing 'If my friends could see me now...'

'And a smile,' Matthew added. 'That's one thing I can't do anything about. Your smile is all your own.'

He began to steer her out of the hotel. The

evening air was heavy with the scent of flowers and spices. Lights were beginning to come on, somewhere a piano was being played, sad tinkling notes of a Noel Coward melody.

Outside the pink stone hotel stood an open white Rolls-Royce, its chromium polished to mirrored perfection, its cream leather seats upholstered for comfort.

Joanna blinked. The evening was turning into some kind of dream. The dinner date, the dress and now a Rolls? Of course, she had forgotten that Matthew was immensely rich; that his percentage on *Planet Eleven* was piling up faster than he could spend it.

Matthew caught Joanna's inquiring expression.

'Yes, the Rolls is mine, but I've changed my mind about using it.' Matthew tossed the keys to the doorman. 'Will you get someone to put it in the garage?' he asked. 'You know, that Rolls used to belong to a maharajah.'

He raised his hand and clicked his fingers, and as if by magic, a horsedrawn tonga came trotting up the drive, feathers nodding on the horse's head, the canopy jangling with bells and tassels, two brightly embroidered cushions on the worn red leather seats. The driver grinned hugely, his few remaining teeth gleaming against his lined face, his crimson turban rakishly askew.

Matthew made sure Joanna was safely seated before speaking to the driver.

'The Amber Palace restaurant,' he said. 'And take it slowly. We aren't out to break any records.'

'Yes, sahib, certainly sahib, very slow,' said the driver, his horse nodding in agreement. 'Very nice tour of Delhi. No extras, you see.'

Matthew settled himself back in the seat, and slipped an arm behind Joanna. 'I had a feeling we would get a tour. Don't be alarmed, Joanna ... this gesture of affection is just in case the driver makes an emergency stop. I hope you are not disappointed about the Rolls. I kept thinking about all those poor folk, living on the streets of Old Delhi, and I just found it damned impossible to drive by them in a monstrous huge car eating up gallons of petrol, going to a meal that will cost more than they'd ever earn in a year, maybe a lifetime. I don't know...'

Joanna wondered if her confused thoughts showed in her eyes. This new side of Matthew had taken her by surprise. She had thought him callous and insensitive, but he had seen the poverty and it had affected him.

'Even if I gave them every cent I earn, it wouldn't make any difference,' he went on, almost talking to himself. 'Sorry, end of sermon.'

The tonga began to move sedately down the drive and out into the main roadway. Outside waited a cluster of motorcycle taxis and bicycle rickshaws. And the beggars, pathetically

36

deformed people, some on little trollies, held their hands out, eyes rimmed with cataract, skin covered in sores ...

Matthew emptied his pockets. Even the most feeble of the cripples suddenly became quite agile, scurrying around for coins in the dust.

They talked very little on that evening ride around Old Delhi and New Delhi. Matthew seemed content to sit back and look at all the strange sights and sounds. Occasionally he pointed something out to Joanna ... street side barbers squatting on the pavements with clients covered in lather ... the letter-writers, with long beards, sitting on the pavements with their equipment laid out before them. Some had ancient and battered typewriters. It was time for the evening meal, and hundreds of charcoal fires burned for cooking, and the pungent smell of curry and spices wafted from these street kitchens. The sugar cane sellers were doing a roaring trade, pushing the cane through their mangle-like contraptions, squeezing the juice into wooden bowls. The customers jostled to buy the sweet drink.

Cinema adverts shone brightly, the glamorous stars smiling mysteriously from the hoardings, giant faces darkly handsome and adored. Building and demolition seemed to be going on side by side, the precarious wooden scaffolding hardly looked adequate for the new buildings replacing the old. Fragile balconies of old colonial homes, now lost in the city, added unexpected touches of faded elegance.

Faded shrines appeared everywhere, fresh and withered flowers lay offered to the gods, perhaps a candle fluttering in the evening breeze. The saffron clad holy men walked through the crowds with their bowls, shaven heads glistening, robes blowing round their sandalled feet. A hermit sat in a conclave of stones and corrugated iron, cross-legged, wrapped in a dirty loin cloth. He had been there for years. People brought him food.

There was a commotion going on in a narrow alley, and as they passed by, Matthew touched Joanna's arm to draw her attention to the noise. Two huge Brahma bulls were charging each other, their horns locked, scattering passersby and the vegetables from a nearby stall.

'Can you imagine such a scene in London or New York?' said Matthew. 'But I think it's time we ate.' He leaned forward and tapped the driver. 'The Amber Palace restaurant now.'

The driver grinned. 'Yes, sahib,' and turned the horse deftly in the opposite direction.

Joanna began to feel alarmed at the rickety speed, but Matthew reached out for her hand and took it firmly.

'The days of wine and roses are short, my darling Joanna, so you might as well enjoy them,' he said. He lifted her fingers to his lips and touched them lightly.

The dark blue eyes were no longer hostile; he was looking at her with a strange expression. There was a warmth about his lazy smile that had not been there before.

Joanna tried to collect her senses. A millionaire, a Rolls Royce, a beautiful dress, dining in a palace ... she was being fed and watered before the slaughter, or seduction. Matthew, so smooth and polished, sitting beside her, kissing her fingers. This was probably a re-run of a hundred such evenings.

'Did you buy the dress to match the restaurant?' she asked mildly.

'No, I chose the restaurant to match you. I thought perhaps my ice princess might melt in such exquisite surroundings. It was once a real palace, built by a rich maharajah for a woman he loved very much. It was rumoured that she was a white woman, brought to India as a slave. Now it is a restaurant; a better fate than being bull-dozed to the ground for offices.'

It was a small palace, set in quiet gardens by the Yamuna river. A beautiful fretstone archway and four slender minarets topped with gold, each looking too fragile to have lasted so many years, made a discreet entrance to the interior, a cool marble hall in shades of amber. The ceiling was ornately inlaid with semi-precious stones. Soft rugs and carpets protected an exquisitely tiled floor from modern shoes.

They were shown into the main saloon

where once the white woman had waited for her foreign prince. But now it was air conditioned and the diners sat at tables so far spaced, and surrounded by banks of flowers, that each was at an island of their own.

'I would have booked an alcove,' said Matthew, guiding Joanna to the far side of the room. 'But I did not want you to get the wrong idea.'

Joanna glanced into one of the alcoves. It was really three rooms, with elaborately carved archways. The first was set with a table, snowy linen, silver cutlery, flowers, gilt chairs. The second was marble floored with two couches, low polished table, and of all things, hanging from the ceiling on silken ropes, was a swing ... beyond that was a third room and Joanna glimpsed a low divan piled high with dozens of cushions almost obliterating the view through doors into the garden.

Joanna knew that her entrance through the saloon had not gone unnoticed. She did not know how to describe it ... not a stir, but more a definite recognition of approval that said her appearance enhanced the beauty of the place itself.

'Everyone has noticed you,' said Matthew with some satisfaction. 'They are all wondering who you are ... perhaps some starlet for my next film.'

'Heaven forbid,' said Joanna. 'I could no more act in a film than stand on my head.'

'I know that,' said Matthew crisply. 'You are totally transparent. Never try to fool me and never lie to me. I can see right through you.'

Three white-tunicked stewards arrived with iced water which they poured into crystal goblets; then a chilled amber wine that reflected mellow highlights; balls of melon were served in crystal dishes that sat in silver bowls that stood on silver dishes. The melon balls were dyed different colours with fruit juices and the edge was decorated with mint leaves curled to look like flowers.

'The rich pay others to make food that tempts their jaded palates,' said Matthew, almost scornfully. 'It's really just a slice of melon tarted up. I have ordered for us. But if you really want to wade through a menu a yard long, you're welcome.'

'No, I'm sure what you've ordered will be fine,' said Joanna. 'It beats a Fleet Street café any day.'

He laughed, that short deep sound that was so attractive. 'I'm glad the practical Miss Hamilton still has her feet planted firmly on mother earth. Takes more than a palace to sweep you off your feet, does it?'

'I wasn't aware that the idea was to sweep me off my feet,' said Joanna. 'I thought we were going to discuss the filming schedules and the plans for the next few days.'

'Were we?' He sounded all innocence. 'Ah,

41

so we were...' He reached into his inside pocket and drew out some sheets of paper. 'I've had my ideas typed up by the secretarial bureau at the hotel. Take a glance at them.'

Joanna firmly squashed the tiny feeling of disappointment that came with the business-like change in his voice. So it had, after all, been planned as a working meal, despite all the trimmings. It would probably go down as expenses, she thought drily. She fingered a little amber elephant on the table. It had a sad, sweet face, holding a single flower in the howdah on its back.

'No, I shall pay for this myself,' said Matthew. 'And the water is safe to drink. There, I said I could read your face.'

They began to discuss the filming and Joanna had to admit that his ideas were good. He planned to see aspects of India through Mandy's eyes, then suddenly to switch to India's view of Mandy herself. Yes, it was a very unusual idea, if it worked. But that was Matthew's problem. She had her own.

'What's the big sigh for? Don't you like my inside-outside India? Can you think of anything better?'

'No, that's the trouble,' said Joanna. 'I can't think of anything at all.' This afternoon she would never have told Matthew Howard her misgivings, but the delicious amber wine was making her feel more relaxed. They had just finished eating tiny scraps of white lobster flesh in a cold and creamy curry sauce, and the stewards were waiting to clear.

'It wasn't meant to be me at all,' Joanna began quite incoherently. 'Nancy Rees Owen was supposed to do the trip. She would have written something witty and sophisticated and extremely clever, even about Mandy. She's that kind of person. Very talented. I've taken her place, because she caught mumps.'

'Mumps?'

'A few little swellings and I stand a good chance of losing my job if I don't come up with some ideas soon.'

'Are you too proud to accept a hand-out?'

'A hand-out?' Joanna was puzzled.

'A suggestion from someone else?'

'It depends how it is offered to me,' said Joanna with spirit. 'Suggestions can be constructive or destructive.'

'Let me think about it. I'm certainly not going to spoil our next course by talking shop. It's a rather famous dish called Shah Jehani pullao, and apparently takes all day to prepare. It wouldn't be fair to spoil such dedication.'

Shah Jehani pullao was tender, succulent pieces of lamb laid on a bed of spiced saffron rice, garnished with raisins and nuts and sprinkled with rose water.

'It should be finally decorated with strips of beaten silver,' said Matthew. 'But I thought this ostentatious and settled for the cheaper dish.'

He began to amuse her with LA gossip, and his rather acid view of Hollywood and its glamour image. It did not sound as if he liked living there. Joanna enjoyed this conversation; she had a reporter's avid curiousity about people and places, and Matthew as a table companion was excellent company.

They finished with a fig sorbet served with slices of fresh nectarine, something that Joanna would never have ordered in a million years. But the slightly tart nectarines were perfect with the sweetness of the fig.

'That,' said Joanna, fighting off a yawn ... 'was a gorgeous meal. Thank you.'

'I was going to suggest coffee in the garden, but I think I'm going to take you straight back to the hotel, before you fall asleep.'

'I'm so sorry, but I am suddenly terribly tired.' Joanna was having difficulty in keeping her eyes open. The long flight, the good food, the wine were all taking their toll.

They began to leave. The stewards darted forward to move their chairs. Matthew stood up and casually picked up the little amber elephant and put it in his pocket. Joanna was horrified.

'Put it on my bill, will you?' he said. 'Madam would like a souvenir.'

As they left the Amber Palace, a beautiful young girl came forward, all smiles, and gave Joanna an orchid. An amber orchid, of course. The night was starry, warm and musky.

Matthew had apparently ordered a car to take them back to the hotel. It was waiting for them with a uniformed driver. Joanna was glad to see it was not one of the rattle-trap taxis, but an elderly limousine.

'Have you thought of anything yet?' she yawned again.

'Let me sleep on it,' he said. 'I promise to come up with an idea tomorrow.'

This driver was slow and careful and before Joanna could stop herself, she was sliding against Matthew and resting her head against his arm. All sorts of delicious thoughts were curling through her mind and she let them come and go, glad not to be talking any more, but just drifting on the shores of sleep …

Matthew looked down at her sleeping face, almost child-like and trustful now. It seemed a pity to wake her.

She hardly stirred as he lifted her out of the car, her head falling against his shoulder. She was very light for a tall girl, and Matthew strode up the steps as if he was carrying a child, the amber chiffon flowing from his arms.

There were very few people to see them so late at night, and they could not see her face turned against his shoulder.

The lift-boy averted his eyes. His were also heavy with sleep.

Matthew shifted Joanna slightly so that he could unlock the door of her room. He half smiled as he saw the linen frock on the floor and the overturned sandals.

Gently he laid her on the bed and took the pins out of her hair. Then he removed her gold mesh mules, and with some difficulty drew the voluminous folds of chiffon over her head. He covered her with a sheet, checked the windows, and then moved away to the door to leave.

'Darling ...?' she murmured, a soft sigh coming from her lips.

'Joanna?' He came to the side of the bed, looking down at her face lit by the rays of slanting moonlight.

A soft young arm crept round his neck, pulling down his face.

'G'night...' she said, all muzzy and lost in sleep. He felt a small moist kiss planted somewhere on his cheek. 'G'night,' she said again, and then she slipped back on the pillow, giving in at last to waves of exhaustion that took her to nirvana.

CHAPTER THREE

It was already quite late when they set out in a fleet of scooter taxis along Mathura road to the Delhi Zoological Gardens.

Mandy had been reluctant to leave the security of the de luxe hotel and lingered so much over her breakfast on the balcony of her room, that Joanna wondered if the girl was going to be ill.

The breakfast was simple but deliciously appropriate for the heat that was building up each hour they waited ... Indian breads, the chappati and richer flaky paratha, little souffles called poories, kachori and pappars; superb fruit, pears, mangoes and guavas; very hot tea with milk or limes. But Mandy did not like any of it. She wanted rice crispies and a milk shake. When the milk shake came, she turned up her pert nose at it.

'This milk tastes funny,' she complained.

Joanna was in no mood to pamper the girl any further. Of course, the milk would taste different. It might be goat's milk, buffalo or buttermilk, tinned or dried. She could hardly ask the hotel to import an English cow.

Joanna had enough to think about as she sipped the fragrant tea, letting the early morning breeze cool her bare arms. When she had awoken, to find herself in bed, she had no recollection how she got there. She remembered little of the drive home, only the overwhelming sense of tiredness. Had Mandy put her to bed? Or had she struggled there herself, so comatose that her actions had been those of a sleep-walker? The alternative, that Matthew had put her to bed, brought a rush of embarrassment and humiliation. He probably thought, if it had been him, that the wine had gone to her head, and she had passed out.

Whatever happened, she was not going to

ask him. Play it cool was today's motto. She had hung the amber chiffon away in her wardrobe but not before Mandy had seen it.

'That's nice,' she said. 'I didn't know you had any nice clothes,' she added with the tactlessness of youth. 'Can I borrow it?'

'It's going back,' said Joanna briefly.

At the zoo they finally met the rest of the film crew. Andre Herriot, the cameraman, was another French-Canadian; a stooped, grey-haired man with lines etched on his face that said a lot about the slight limp he tried to hide. He had a stick which he tucked away each time he hoisted the camera onto his shoulder.

'Of course, it would be a pleasure to take some still shots of the delightful mademoiselle. You have only to say what you want,' he said.

'Anything,' said Joanna. 'Just anything will be fine.'

The woman was Lucille Boardman. Joanna had read of her on the gossip pages. She changed husbands almost as often as she changed her wardrobe. She went from one rich man to another, her attorney untangling the legal knots with practised ease.

Her face was quite unmarked. Emotional traumas had left her unscathed. She was the kind of elegant American woman that made Joanna feel that her own clothes were all jumble sale bargains.

She came over to Joanna accompanied by the jangling of the collection of gold bracelets she wore on her thin wrist. Perhaps they were a walking dowry.

'Miss Hamilton? I'm Lucille Boardman. I assist Matthew Howard.'

The smile was glossy but it did not stretch to the eyes hidden behind tinted glasses. It was impossible to see the colour of her eyes, or detect their true expression.

'How do you do?' said Joanna. 'Joanna Hamilton of the *Daily Post*. I'm in charge of our Magic Carpet winner.'

'Oh no,' said Lucille with a tinkling laugh. 'Matthew is in charge. That's the first thing you'll learn when we're filming. And when we're not filming. Matthew is the big boss. And I'm his number two.'

Joanna did not argue. Those long, crimson varnished talons waving in the air looked lethal. But she set her jaw. Joanna could be stubborn too.

It did not surprise Joanna to learn later that Lucille's ex-husband had been one of the men who had backed Matthew Howard's talent before the days of *Planet Eleven*. Lucille, who had more than enough money to keep her idling on the play beaches of the world, wanted to be a film director herself. She had attached herself to Matthew, prepared to learn at the feet of the master.

Joanna thought how neatly Matthew had organised the cast of this particular slice of life drama. Lucille was making it quite clear to

49

everyone that Matthew and she had a special wavelength going which no one could share. Pierre was already talking Mandy out of her early morning sulks, for which Joanna was duly grateful. She was glad that Mandy had a nice young man for companionship.

And was the mature, father-like Andre Herriot supposed to partner her?

'Hello,' said Matthew. 'Sleep well?' It was as if the Amber Palace had never been. The question had been tossed at her in passing. 'Level up there, Andre.'

'Blissfully,' she said. She was not going to ask him how she got there. 'I shall be returning the dress,' she added.

'Naturally,' he said, not even looking at her. 'A lady of your class would not be expected to wear a dress more than once.'

They filmed Mandy with a lion cub, a black swan and then a monkey on a lead. She was nervous of the lion cub, terrified of the swan and horrified by the monkey's habits.

'And it smells revolting,' she complained, as its bright little eyes blinked at her, and its tiny brown fingers clutched her ra-ra skirt. 'Let go ...' she squirmed.

But Joanna found herself loving it. She approved of the way the animals, even the big ones like the huge horned rhinoceros and heavy bodied hippopotamus, roamed free against a natural background in spacious enclosures. Deep ditches separated people

50

from the animals. And again, there were so many people.

The elephant rides looked fun; the rare white tigers were spectacular creatures; and the gardens were overrun with wild grey and silver striped chipmunks that raced across the paths and darted among the branches, playing hide and seek with the visitors. Lizards scuttled along stone walls, darting, then freezing.

They gave her a milk-sated and sleepy golden lion cub to hold in her arms, and the baby purred like a kitten. It was a heart-strings moment, all tugs and twangs of maternal stirrings. Joanna laughed unconsciously, not knowing that the camera was on her.

How was she going to convey all these rich sights and sounds to her readers, she wondered. One needed to be a poet to capture this elusive timelessness, the splendours of the past that had crumbled before the Early Briton had even discovered woad.

She liked watching Matthew work. His eyes were narrowed with concentration; he moved fast, made decisions fast, and yet every shot was carefully planned. So far, this morning, she had not stepped on his toes.

They went on to Rajghat, the gardens by the river Yamuna, where Mahatma Gandhi's body was cremated.

'How peaceful it is here,' said Joanna. 'Gandhi was assassinated on a Friday, so every Friday they hold a ceremony here in his memory.'

'I've never heard of him,' said Mandy, bored. 'My feet hurt.'

'He was the father of modern India. You should have worn comfortable sandals instead of those stilts.'

'It's all tombs, tombs, tombs,' Mandy said, getting out her lipstick. 'Tombs and monuments and ruins, and flies. I've never seen so many flies. I'm sick of them.'

The temperature was beginning to soar towards mid-day and everyone decided it was back to the Ashoka for a swim and perhaps some lunch. Mandy immediately cheered up, especially when Pierre suggested lunching at the Rambles, at Connaught Place, where they could watch the famous Connaught Circus.

'I will return your Magic Carpet girl quite safely,' said Pierre, seeing Joanna's reluctance.

They waved as Pierre helped Mandy into a tonga. Joanna remembered the drive with Matthew ... had it been a dream? She might not even exist, for all the notice Matthew had taken of her this morning. Last night had obviously been a buttering-up exercise, and duly buttered, she was now being made to realise her place.

Back at the hotel, Joanna escaped to her room and changed into a low-backed black swimsuit. This was one of her extravagant purchases, being perfectly cut, with a spider's web of straps across the bare back.

52

The water was warm, yet beautifully cool compared to the outside air temperature. She swam slowly and lazily, enjoying the first swim of the year for her, a very unaccustomed pleasure for her in a busy London life. She heard a heavy splash in the deep end, and then the swift cutting of the water as someone swam the length with a fast crawl.

Leaves rustled on the tall trees stretching sky-wards, and the birds hopped and twittered among the branches. She felt her irritation at Mandy's unco-operative behaviour washing away with the water that slid smoothly over the skin of her bare shoulders and along her bare legs.

The fast swimmer was crawling alongside Joanna now, his arms splashing in time with her more sedate side-stroke.

'I see your problem,' said Matthew. 'One morning's work with Miss Robbins, and I'm glad I have a camera. She's hardly inspiring material when her eyes are fixed like a limpet on young Pierre.'

His voice cut through her quiet thoughts, bringing her back to the present. She had met Bruce one summer's day, swimming in a lake fringed with weeping willows ...

Matthew stopped swimming, water pouring off his face, his lashes stuck with droplets, the glint of gold reflecting among the dark hair on his wet chest. It was as if he was standing in a shower, and Joanna felt all the attraction of his

53

lean brown body. There was no spare flesh on him. It was all muscle, strong and broad, glistening now with the water and sun mingling on his skin.

Joanna deliberately sank into the water so that it was up to her neck. She did not want him doing a similar evaluation of her boyish figure.

'Where's this great idea for me?' she asked. 'More difficult than you thought?'

'Not at all,' he said, swiftly. 'It came to me straight away. Mandy is desperately trying not to show that she is out of her depth, that's why she latches onto any young man in sight. She's not happy, so she's rude. She needs careful and sympathetic handling.'

'Are you trying to tell me that I'm not sympathetic, or careful?' Joanna objected to his remark. 'I'm doing everything I can for the girl. Perhaps you'd like to fetch and carry for her, and hang up her clothes. The fuss there was this morning, just about getting up. And nothing was right about breakfast.'

'Calm down, lady. I was not accusing you of anything but dedication to your job. I was just suggesting that you go easy on her. She's very young and probably homesick.'

'All right,' said Joanna, taking a deep breath and bobbing up. 'I'll try, I'll try. But I don't accept that it's my fault. Mandy is a very difficult girl.'

'I ordered some iced coffee,' said Matthew. 'I see it's just arrived. Would you like to join me?'

He climbed out of the pool, then leaned over to help Joanna. Two tall glasses stood in silver holders, straws emerging from the pale froth at the top. He held a chair out for her, then slipped his white bath robe over her shoulders.

'You are quite right to be careful about burning,' he said, almost kindly, then spoilt it by adding: 'Or are you worried that I will look at your legs?'

Joanna wrapped the robe across her knees. It was a beautiful fabric, a velvet towelling, soft and absorbent.

'Not everyone has a year-round LA tan,' she said with some spirit. 'Some people stay in England and pay their taxes.'

She saw a small muscle beside his mouth tighten. His eyes darkened dangerously, and she realised she had gone too far.

'That's hitting below the belt,' he said. 'I told you, I live where the work is. I've paid more in tax to the British Government than you could possibly hope to earn in a couple of lifetimes. I practically pick up the tab for the defence budget on my own.'

Joanna could not help a little half laugh. She bit her lower lip. 'Sorry,' she said. 'I say things without thinking.'

'That's what I like about you,' he said surprisingly. 'You are totally honest. You don't grovel. You're not after my money, trying to get a part in my next film, wanting to

55

get into my bed. It makes a change.'

She felt the colour rising in her cheeks, and hid her face over the glass of iced coffee, sucking up the pale froth. 'This is delicious,' she murmured.

'Have I embarrassed you?' he said, stirring the liquid with a straw. 'Do you want to come in to my bed?'

'Madly,' she quipped lightly. She wished he would change the subject. She was used to the banter of a newspaper office, but not with a man like Matthew Howard.

'Eleven thirty then, and don't be late. I don't like women who are late.'

'Do I knock three times and ask for Matty?' she joked, but there was a tremor in her voice which he detected immediately. He leaned across the table and tilted her chin with one finger. He seemed to be taking her wet face to pieces, looking at every contour, every lash, every imperfection. It was utterly unnerving, yet Joanna could not move away. Suddenly he let go and sat back.

'Don't worry,' he said. 'I only go for voluptuous movie starlets. You can feel quite safe.'

It was insulting. Joanna longed to get up and walk away but she needed Matthew's help; she could not afford to alienate him completely; and her legs felt so weak that she doubted if they would have carried her with dignity.

But it was Matthew who stood up. 'I have to

make a phone call,' he said. 'It's the Red Fort this afternoon. Try to get your Magic Carpet girl there on time. We'll go ahead to make the arrangements and take some background film.'

Silently Joanna handed him back his bath robe. He could not walk through the hotel in wet swimming shorts.

'I take it though that I do have to beg for this idea,' she said coolly. 'Perhaps you would like me to go down on my knees? I am getting tired of asking.'

'Don't tempt me. The idea of the haughty Joanna Hamilton on her knees has its possibilities. I am sure you would look very fetching. Wait for me. I'll be back in five minutes.'

But Joanna was not waiting for anyone, especially Matthew Howard. He seemed to think he could just order her around as if she were part of his crew. He could keep his ideas. She would think up something for herself.

Mandy returned after her lunch, hot and sticky and reluctant to do any more sightseeing. She was tired of India already. It was all far too strange, too foreign, for her to adjust to. She wanted to go home. It had all been very exciting at first; the publicity and the lovely clothes; telling all her friends. But the reality was quite different. It was not exciting at all. The filming was like work, being told to do this and that. She hated the heat and the flies.

'Matthew Howard is expecting us at three, so we have to go,' said Joanna firmly. 'If he gets the shots he wants quickly, then you can come back and spend the rest of the afternoon by the pool. Now have a quick shower and put on something pretty.'

'I don't like any of the clothes,' Mandy grumbled. 'They are all urghk. I wouldn't be seen dead in them at home.'

'Would you like to telephone your parents?' Joanna suggested, remembering Matthew's remarks.

'I expect they'll all be out,' said Mandy, kicking off her shoes. 'They're always out. My mum works for my uncle. They run a decorating business. I do the office work sometimes.'

Joanna glanced at Mandy's dejected face. There was a droop to her shoulders as she huddled in a chair, rubbing her feet. The tight shoes had left red marks on her toes. It would have been so easy to go over to the girl and put a sisterly arm round her, but Joanna hesitated, and the moment passed.

Swarms of child beggars converged on them as they arrived in the forecourt of the Red Fort. The driver shouted at them, and the children scattered in all directions, clutching their rags and their deformities. A small boy, covered in sores and more persistent than the others, whined hoarsely at Mandy's elbow, holding out a grubby palm. Mandy shuddered and turned away in distaste.

Joanna dropped some coins into his hand. She pushed Mandy quickly through the covered passageway that led through the massive sandstone walls of the defence barbican which surrounded the seventh city of the Delhi of Shah Jahan. They ignored the outstretched hands of the beggars lying along the base of the wall. The tunnel was cool and dark; it smelled of centuries of ceremony and power. It was not difficult to imagine the richly decorated elephants and the Moghul princes riding in golden howdahs passing through the main gateway to the palace beyond.

They came out into blinding sunshine and before them lay the whole citadel—marble pavilions and mosques, the royal baths, formal gardens, dry and dusty watercourses, a magnificence of marble against spacious green lawns and the dazzling blue sky. The pure white marble of the Pearl Mosque, where the court ladies had once lived, was a confection of ornate decoration.

Mandy immediately spotted the souvenir shops that lined the walks.

'Let's look at the shops,' said Joanna, seeing the sound and vision team moving towards them. They wandered along the open-fronted stalls looking at beautifully embroidered evening bags, traditional jewellery, fabulous silks and brocades, brass and silverware.

Mandy suddenly saw thousands of coloured bangles hung in gaudy rows, and was easily persuaded by an alert shopkeeper to find her size. There were plain bangles, patterned enamelled, silver, gold. The choice was endless.

Joanna stopped to rest on a low, stone wall. The watercourses which had been so elaborately laid out in the gardens were now empty and dried up. How refreshing the sound of running water in the channels had been for those far off emperors, who relied only on water and cunningly caught breezes to temper the summer heat. No air conditioning or refrigerators for them, thought Joanna, not envying their life despite the riches.

Seven years I've been doing this, thought Joanna, watching Mandy pushing a dozen bangles along her arm. Seven years of writing about other people's lives, to record other people's weddings, romances, luck ... the pools win, stardom, top of the pops, legacies, the runaway heiress, Gretna Green. She was always the spectator, never the person it happened to.

The sun threw long blue shadows into the covered shopping bazaar. Joanna sniffed at the mixed scents of fresh jasmine, hair oil and sticky sweetmeats. She wondered whether to buy a carved bullock or elephant for her flat in London.

Andre Herriot propped his stick upright, and leaned against the wall, making sure his camera was safe.

'I am getting too old for this walking in the heat,' he said, taking out a handkerchief to mop his forehead. 'But there is so much to see. These emperors were artists, weren't they?'

'Is it painful for you?' Joanna asked.

'Sometimes,' he said abruptly.

She kicked herself for asking. Always the reporter, always intruding. Pierre was moving his equipment to catch the conversation of Mandy and the shopkeeper. She was a born haggler. She wanted a lot of bangles and she wanted a bargain. She was wearing mauve culottes in crepe de chine, with a striped sailor top, very trendy and enchanting. Her eyes sparkled as she battled for a good price.

Joanna gazed up into the cloudless sky, the brilliant sun cutting a sharp pattern of leaves across her face. The ever present chipmunks scampered across a dusty path and up some dry bark.

'You are tired, mademoiselle?'

'I'm not used to the heat yet.'

'Sound running,' said Pierre.

'It is strange to think that all this is quite new when compared with the other Indian dynasties,' said Andre, his hand sweeping the vista of intricately carved mosques and pavilions.

'Indian history is totally confusing,' said Joanna. 'I've given up trying to work it out. I'm sitting here determined to print these breathtakingly beautiful views on my mind, so that when I'm back in London, rattling along in a crowded bus, I'll be able to do an instant replay.'

'How very wise,' Andre smiled. 'I will mount a montage for you also, so that you will also have something special to look at on foggy days in your capital.'

Joanna did not tell him that London's pea-soupers were a thing of the past. She smiled and thanked him. He was being very kind. Matthew Howard obviously picked people of an unusual genre for his team. Perhaps that was why he was so successful. The way they worked together, each contributing something special, lifted the finished product into a class of its own.

She knew she was going to fail. Perhaps they would not even print a word of what she wrote. Mr Wilberforce would spike the lot, and all the money the *Daily Post* had spent, the publicity, the promotion, the prize money, would all be wasted. Someone would have to be sacrificed and she had no doubt that it would be her head on the block. Farewell, Miss Hamilton. Back to the provinces.

She wandered over to a stall, pretending to be interested in its wares, but really hiding her momentary anxiety. The turbaned shopkeeper rushed to her side, producing a dozen further items to catch her attention.

'All very good, very cheap,' he insisted.

'Look at this, missy. Little red bean. Very lucky. Let me show you. Wait, please...'

With nicotine-stained fingers he found the nail-fine crack and opening the bean, shook it gently. Something like a fine white ash fell out and scattered over the black cloth on the counter.

'A hundred elephants!' said the Indian triumphantly. 'Would you believe it? A hundred ivory elephants, each one hand carved. Look, missy. You look, missy.' He thrust a magnifying glass into her hand. 'Each one is an elephant. Pure ivory. Very cheap. Very lucky.'

Joanna peered through the glass at the crude, wafer thin fragments. She could just make out that they were elephants. 'Amazing,' she said, not wanting to hurt his obvious pride. 'I need some luck. I need some luck very badly.'

'We could both do with some luck.'

Matthew was standing beside her, peeling dirty rupee notes from a roll. 'Two lucky red beans,' he said to the shopkeeper. 'No need to count the elephants. I'll take your word for it.'

'Both beans will bring you astounding luck,' said the shopkeeper, wrapping the beans in a scrap of brown paper. 'You will see, sahib. You will be back. All your family will want lucky red beans. Thank you. Thank you.'

Matthew pocketed the twisted scrap of paper and turned to Joanna.

'You didn't wait for me,' he said.

63

'I too had a phone call to make,' she said after an uncomfortable pause.

'Liar. Don't lie to me. I told you, I can see it in your face.'

'I knew Mandy would be back from her lunch with Pierre, and I had to make sure she would be ready for this afternoon,' Joanna amended.

He took her arm, almost roughly, his fingers gripping the bare skin, and steered her away from the stall and away from the others.

'You are bruising me,' she flared at him. 'Please let go of my arm.'

He turned her to face him. They were standing beneath the sweeping branches of a fiery gold laburnum tree, the heavy clusters of flowers moving in the breeze, the air full of scents and small rustling sounds of the secret animals that lived within the branches.

'I've a good mind not to tell you how to write Mandy's Diary. You don't deserve any help at all. I should leave you to flounder in heavy paragraphs of descriptive prose, wallow in architectural detail, drown in Indian historical facts. When all the time your *Daily Post* readers are longing to know what Mandy had for breakfast; what she did not want to wear; how many flies she swotted.'

She could not tell whether he was being kind, or still more hateful. Why did he take such a delight in this verbal cruelty, this lashing with words? It was unnerving.

Joanna moistened her lips. She longed, more than anything, for a long cool safe drink ... bland barley water, bitter lemon, even a glass of water from an English tap.

'You mean each day in a diary form as if Mandy had written it? No poetry, no prose. Just her own blunt words ... 9 a.m. breakfast, the buffalo milk is revolting; 10 a.m. hair-raising ride on a scooter taxi. I thought we would crash. 3 p.m. The Red Fort, it is so hot I could die. That's awful ...' sighed Joanna.

'You are not looking at what is giving her pleasure,' said Matthew. 'All your three examples were the negative side. Didn't you watch her trying on bangles and haggling over the price? Did you ask her what she thought of Connaught Place? I bet they even do a curried hamburger. Think about it, Joanna. It has the merit of being brief. It could be eye-catching. Very readable. Funny. And if you are determined to wax lyrical, then each day you could add a footnote, a boxed item, today's five-star special: What Mandy Didn't See or What Mandy Missed. A view, a sunset, a ruin ... something that has caught your heart strings but which means nothing to her.'

Joanna began to see the possibilities. It might catch their readers' fancy, and the *Daily Post* was always short of space.

'Mandy had her fortune told in Connaught Place today, by a fortune teller with a long beard. He told her that she was loved by two men—her father and her husband,' Joanna mused. 'I suppose I could use that.'

'I think you're getting the idea. It's good and it'll work, and I'm sure you could write it well.'

It was the first time Matthew had said anything remotely encouraging about her work. She was afraid to feel grateful; he seemed to generate such power over people and she had no intention of joining the admiring throng.

'My double thanks,' she said, faintly mocking. 'For the compliment—unexpected but nevertheless always acceptable. And for the diary idea. I'll have a word with my editor, but I have a feeling he'll go for it. I hope you won't expect a by-line.'

'Just another kiss.' He threw the remark at her as he turned back to the group. 'Last night's kiss was juvenile, but fairly pleasant. Unexpected, but nevertheless acceptable.'

Joanna stared after him. His white shirt was clinging to his back in wet patches, his hips moved with the grace and strength of a panther. He was head and shoulders taller than the much shorter Indians. Even the Indian women glanced at him shyly, some drawing a gauzy veil across their faces to hide their boldness.

What kiss? All her misgivings about the evening and her arrival in bed came flooding back. What had happened? Had she drunk too much of that delicious amber wine? She wanted to know what she had done that seemed to amuse him . . . Joanna shivered at the thought of kissing Matthew at all, and like a schoolgirl, it seemed. How foolish she had been, even to go out with him.

'Have we finished Delhi?' Mandy was asking.

'Finished?' Lucille looked scandalised. 'Delhi has about a thousand historical monuments. We've hardly started.'

The way Mandy's face fell was almost comical.

'Come in quickly on focus,' said Matthew, seeing her expression.

'Don't be alarmed,' said Pierre, coming to the rescue. 'No one could possibly see everything. We shall only visit some of the most outstanding ones.'

'Do I talk posh enough for this film?' she asked. 'If not, I can soon go home. I don't mind, you know. I've got plenty to do. In fact, I'm missing several quite important engagements.'

'But this is also an important engagement,' said Pierre, packing up his equipment. 'Remember, you are going to be a star.' His eyes twinkled. They were a pleasant soft brown, clear and uncomplicated, so different from the brooding dark blue eyes of his employer. 'You may even become famous!' Mandy's edginess subsided with the young man's encouraging small talk.

'I thought we'd go and see some classical dancing,' said Matthew. 'There's a performance of Kathak dancing this evening.'

Mandy brightened. She loved dancing. 'Good,' she said. 'I fancy going dancing. I hope they've got all the latest hits.'

Joanna despaired, but did not enlighten the girl. 'You don't know when you're lucky,' she murmured.

Matthew took Joanna's hand and pressed something into the palm. The movement was so quick that no one noticed.

Joanna did not uncurl her fingers. She knew what he had given her. A lucky red bean with a hundred elephants.

CHAPTER FOUR

They were marooned in what Joanna could only describe as a picturesque traffic jam. Despite the blaring hooters and hysterical arguments, it was a good-humoured jam, without any of the tension of London traffic hold-ups. Somewhere ahead a string of donkeys, laden with fodder, plodded through the heavy traffic. Every other vehicle—taxis, scooters, bullock carts, horse-drawn tongas— had slowed to the donkeys' pace. Only the hordes of cyclists could slip through the gaps.

All six of them had squashed into the same

ancient limousine which Matthew and Joanna had ridden in from the Amber Palace. A second car which he had requested had not turned up. Andre was sitting in front, next to the chauffeur so that he could stretch out his leg. The three women sat on the back seat, and the two men took the tip-up seats.

Joanna was in the middle, trying to feel cool and relaxed, but the perfume of the older American woman was a heavy musk and quite overwhelming. It was a wonder that Mandy was not complaining, but she was by an open window and in animated conversation with Pierre. Lucille was asking Matthew for his opinion on some technical aspect of the filming, deliberately isolating Joanna.

The bean was still crushed in her hand. She was afraid to open her fingers in case she dropped the tiny thing. What an amazing, unpredictable man ... a gown worth two or three hundred pounds one day, and the next day a touristy souvenir costing fifty pence or so. She knew the cheap and funny gift meant far more to her than the expensive dress.

She could watch him as he talked earnestly with Lucille. His face was even more arresting as he described in detail some new and complicated technique which he had invented. Those eyes were grave and serious now, but there was in his deep voice a controlled enthusiasm that he was holding in check. Joanna knew that she would remember every detail of his features, even if she never saw him again.

Suddenly his eyes switched to her, capturing her look.

It was like an electric shock, as if he had physically reached out to her. Joanna felt her heart quicken, but she could not drag gaze away. Their eyes were locked, but his expression was unfathomable, dark and penetrating, searching her soul.

A sudden jerk broke the glance. The donkeys had turned into a side street bazaar, and the whole stream of traffic threw its gears into top with a burst of revving engines.

'Ye Gods, these drivers,' said Lucille, her heavy gold bracelets jangling as she touched her immaculate hair. Joanna noticed the large brilliant rings and red talons. She wondered if Matthew was thinking of becoming the second husband—or was it third—of this bird of prey. She was a well-preserved forty, using every trick of money and make-up to halt the advancing years. Perhaps her abrasive worldliness appealed to Matthew. But Lucille was not the kind of woman to whom he could give a little red bean ...

Joanna tried to dismiss her foolish thoughts, but the little bean warmed her hand. Her palm was probably red with dye by now, she guessed, a smile hovering on her face. Suddenly she did not care about all these people around her. A calmness came over her.

She felt a completeness, a feeling which had evaded her for years. Whatever happened, she had strength now. She could face anything that life tossed in her path.

But where had it come from ... the magic of the great Mogul palaces and the power long gone, the little red bean, that strange look from Matthew? Perhaps the strength had been there all the time, waiting for her to recognise it.

Matthew was taking the scrap of paper from his pocket, refolding it carefully and placing it in his wallet.

'What's that?' Lucille asked, her eyes darting on the small package with curiosity.

'A talisman,' he said briefly.

'A diamond, emerald?' Lucille knew that Delhi was a major centre for jewellery, goldsmiths and silversmiths. And Matthew could afford anything. She was hoping that he would show her what he had purchased. He might even give it to her.

She put her hand on his arm, smiling up at him with a look of intimacy that did not go unnoticed by Joanna.

'Remember the night of the premiere of *Planet Eleven*?' she said, lowering her voice huskily. 'You gave me a brooch with eleven perfect sapphires. It's still my favourite piece of jewellery.'

'The brooch was a gift from both of us,' Matthew reminded her. 'It came from your husband and me.'

71

'I know who chose it even if he paid for it,' said Lucille, with a little shrug. 'You don't have to tell me who has taste. Oh this awful heat ... the sooner we get back to the States the better. Let's get this crummy two-reeler over and done with. It really isn't worth your time and talent, Matthew.'

'I think it is,' he said. He turned suddenly to Joanna. 'Do you think this trip is worth all our efforts?'

She was taken by surprise, her thoughts elsewhere.

'Yes, it's worth it for the people who'll never have a chance to see India. For half-an-hour, they'll see something of its magic on the box.'

'I hope my film merits more than half-an-hour's showing.'

'Even you have to fit a programme slot,' said Joanna.

'I bow to your superior knowledge,' he said, turning away.

Joanna bit her lip. Why had she said that, when he had just given her a glimpse of a different man? It must be the heat.

'You didn't show me your talisman,' Lucille persisted. 'Is it unique?'

'Something like that,' he said, replacing the wallet in his back pocket. Lucille gave a little mannered pout, and smiled at him through her long feathery lashes. She was too clever to insist that he showed her.

Everyone made plans for an hour by the

72

pool, but not Joanna. She had put off writing her pieces for too long. She had to telephone Mr Wilberforce as soon as the hotel could get a line for her.

She hurried to their suite in the hotel, anxious to put through the call and to find a safe-keeping place for the bean. There was no dye on the palm of her hand, only the print of her nails in the flesh. So it was a real bean after all. Perhaps the hundred elephants were real ivory too.

Mr Wilberforce was still at his desk when Joanna phoned. He listened to Joanna's proposal for Mandy's Diary with some relief. He had had misgivings about sending Joanna on the assignment to the extent that he had Nancy Rees Owen at the ready to re-write Joanna's copy from her bed.

'Joanna, that sounds a great idea,' he said, 'I'm all for it. Neat, economical, and down to earth. Let's have the first copy as soon as you can. Use the telex service. What about the photographs?'

'Andre is putting the first prints on the Air India flight tonight, arriving Heathrow tomorrow mid-morning,' said Joanna.

'Great. Carry on with the good work. And enjoy yourself, Joanna. It might be the only holiday you get this year!'

Joanna sat on the edge of her bed and found that she was quite unsteady. She had been unsure whether Mr Wilberforce would like the idea. It was one hurdle over. And he had even made a little joke . . . that was progress indeed.

Her spirits surged. She knew she could write Mandy's Diary. There would be no difficulty in putting herself in Mandy's shoes and chronicling events in a simple diary style. She remembered the way her heels had sunk into the soft tarmac at the airport; the garlands of marigolds and mimosa, petals spilling on the floor; the first sight of the garden city.

She was working hard at the table on her balcony, when a knock came at the door. A steward came in with a tray of tea, sweet cakes and fruit.

She looked surprised, knowing that she had ordered nothing, though she suddenly realised that she was hungry.

'With compliments of Mr Howard,' he said smoothly, bowing his way out of the suite.

Joanna was touched. She had not eaten since breakfast, and Matthew would know how much energy was required for the concentration of writing.

The hot tea was refreshing and revitalising. As she munched the small sweet cakes, she began to write something else. There were so many sights and sounds, so much contrast in the old and new Delhi, and she had to put it all down. Her pen raced across the paper, making verbal pictures for herself, capturing every sensation of delight and recoil, every scene of humour and pathos. She was exhausted when she had finished, her wrist aching from writing in a cramped position. She hurried down to the hotel's office behind the foyer. All the marvels of modern communication would have her copy on Mr Wilberforce's desk before the paper went to bed that night.

Later she lay in perfumed bath water, dozing as the fatigue slipped from her mind and body. She was thinking how she would thank Matthew. It had been a kind thought, and she wanted him to know that she appreciated it. On the other hand, she did not want him to think she was a little ninny, won over by tea and cakes, like giving sweets to a child.

She heard Mandy singing in her bath, which was a good sign.

They had arranged to meet in the Peacock Room overlooking the gardens, where a small band was playing semi-classical Indian music. Joanna knew she was not looking like an amber goddess this evening, but she had deliberately chosen to look quite different. She was wearing a bright ethnic cotton skirt, and a simple, long-sleeved peasant blouse. She found the air-conditioning in public rooms quite icy, and did not want to spend the evening shivering.

Mandy, for some reason known only to herself, was wearing a white beaded evening dress over a pair of coral beach trousers. She had the dress on back to front, and had twisted the belt through her hair.

Andre and Pierre were waiting for them, the older man leaning on his stick, looking tired, though his face lightened as Joanna approached. Her heart sank. This was to be a foursome. Matthew and Lucille were dining elsewhere.

She forced herself to enjoy the meal and the company of the two French-Canadians. At least she could be herself, and not be wondering all the time if she was doing or saying the right thing. Matthew had an overpowering effect on her confidence.

'I'm going to try the Moghul speciality,' said Joanna, hoping it would not be too hot. 'Spiced, barbecued tandoori chicken. If you see me gasping, please send for the fire brigade.'

'Not me,' said Mandy. 'I can't stand curry. I'll have fish and chips.'

Pierre interpreted this preference as scampi, and ordered for Mandy. What an extraordinarily nice young man, thought Joanna. French charm and Canadian practicality.

'I have two younger sisters at home,' he said, as if having read Joanna's thought. 'Mandy reminds me very much of the youngest.'

'Oh? And what's she like?' Mandy demanded.

'She is like an adorable little kitten,' said Pierre smoothly, half grinning. 'And when she annoys me, I tip her out into the garden.'

'I'd like to see you doing that to me,' Mandy retorted. 'No one is going to boss me about.'

Joanna tried to dismiss Matthew completely from her mind. What did it matter where they were, what they were eating, what they were talking about. Last night had been simply Matthew's way of stamping the trip with his authority.

She tasted the food and yet hardly knew what she was eating. She talked and laughed and contributed to the conversation, and then could not remember a word that had been said. If only they were not going on to the performance of Kathak dancing. It would be nice to have an evening away from Mandy, Matthew and everyone else connected with the Magic Carpet competition.

It was a kind of music, strange to European ears. Two drummers accompanied a sarangi player, an Indian type of violin, and with them was a singer, her voice reproducing the drum syllables. The blades of the fans hummed against the ceiling, stirring the air round the audience in the hall.

Originally a temple dance, the Kathak was now a court dance, and the dancers, both men and women, came onto the floor to begin their programme. Matthew and Lucille had not arrived yet.

It was impossible not to be enchanted by the dancing, as the dancers, with three rows of bells on the anklets they wore, were able to imitate with their feet the exact sound of the drums. Their painted faces were immobile and all the meaning was in their swaying bodies and sensuous movements of their arms.

The silk of their embroidered skirts rustled as the dancers went through their intricate footwork, each dance telling a religious drama or a love story.

The rhythmic beat began to pulse through Joanna's veins and she found herself understanding the woman's poetic plea to her lover. The hastas, or hand gestures, were the alphabet of her love, spelling a rapture that was sensitive and erotic. Joanna felt her longing grow; to find the right man; to find a man with the right balance of strength and wisdom. Perhaps her dream man did not exist, that combination of passion and tenderness, authority and understanding, stature and humility ...

'Waiting for me?' Matthew's voice was low as he slipped into the empty chair beside her. He glanced at her.

'No, we've been here ages,' said Joanna. 'We decided not to wait.' It was infuriating how his arrival beside her could make her feel so ill at ease.

'I hope you are watching this very carefully,' he went on, his tone intimate and teasing. 'You could learn a lot...'

Joanna refused to answer. The dance was superbly exciting and enthralling, but now she could think only of the man sitting casually beside her, his long legs crossed, the toe of his polished shoe tapping in time to the drum beat.

The girl dancer was both demure and wanton, the little bells tinkling on her anklets, her painted eyes and doll-like face raised to the moon like a flower. Her glance rested on Matthew, and for a fleeting moment, her expression was one of invitation.

For a moment Joanna envied the girl's simplicity. She had seen a man she liked; she signalled so. It was uncomplicated.

They grouped together in the vast lounge to have a coffee after the dancing. Pierre and Mandy were going out to a disco.

'No bleary eyes tomorrow,' Matthew warned. 'We're filming early.'

'I'm young. I can dance all night,' said Mandy.

'The tact of the young,' said Lucille, re-arranging a gold and white shawl over her bare, sun-tanned shoulders.

She had the look of a cat who had just been fed a very large saucer of cream. Her white Grecian dress was clinging and expensive; gold jewellery dripped from her arms and fingers.

'Don't take Mandy to the Amber Palace,' she added as they were leaving. 'It's fabulously expensive and absolutely out of this world. It's the most perfect place I've ever seen.'

Matthew was staring at the ceiling, his dark head tilted back. Andre looked from Lucille's smile of satisfaction, to Joanna's frozen face, wondering what had happened.

Lucille was babbling on about the food, the decor, the fantastic chandeliers, the little honeymoon alcoves ... while Joanna fought the tumult in her mind. She had thought the visit to the Amber Palace so special, something laid on just for her, to match her amber gown. Now she knew how foolish she had been, to read something into the evening that had not been there at all. She had been day-dreaming with herself as Cinderella. The Prince, it seemed, took a different girl to the ball each evening.

She took advantage of a short lull in the conversation to excuse herself with a plea of tiredness. It was not an invention; she was worn out by the heat and the complications of the day. She was beginning to feel like Mandy; the sooner it was all over and they could go home, the better.

Once in her room, Joanna did not go to bed. Instead she dragged the sheet off the bed and wrapping it round herself she went and sat on the balcony. There were neon lights in the centre of the city, but the softer yellow glow of flickering oil lamps pin-pointed the smaller streets. From the outskirts of the town she could hear the howl of jackals, a sound weird enough to chill any European.

She knew now that she had been half way to falling in love with Matthew Howard; a stupid, crazy thing to do. He had been playing with her like a fish on a line ... a gift here, a little flattery, then the acid remark, the dismissal, the cutting down to size. Lucille had done her a favour, showing up Matthew's indifference before it was too late.

She was crying. It had hurt. She tried to see the funny side of it ... Joanna Hamilton thinking that the great Matthew Howard was interested in her, even thought she looked beautiful. Joanna failed to make herself smile. It had been a marvellous evening. Perhaps she should just leave it at that, and tuck it away in her memories as being the one evening when she was treated like a princess.

'Too hot for you?' Matthew was speaking to her from his balcony. 'Taken to sleeping outside? Most Indians sleep on their roofs on string beds. It's the coolest place.'

'I was just enjoying the view,' said Joanna, turning her face away so that she could wipe the tears from her cheeks. She had no desire for him to know that she had been crying.

'Wait till you see the Taj Mahal by moonlight. It's breath-taking. The most beautiful sight on earth.'

He vaulted over the partition and strolled across to the empty cane and cushion chair. He sat down, unbuttoning his jacket, as if he had come for a long stay.

'I didn't invite you over,' she said.

'That's right. I invited myself.'

81

'Well, you've got a nerve,' she said. 'I'm just going to bed.'

'Care to join me in a night-cap? It'll soothe your nerves. Help you to sleep?'

'No thank you,' said Joanna, stiffly. 'My nerves don't need soothing.'

'Not true. You are as uptight as a well-tuned piano string. Relax lady ... has young Mandy been playing you up all evening?'

Did she detect a wicked gleam in those dark eyes, as if he quite relished the outbursts and tantrums which Mandy produced so frequently.

'Well, you wouldn't know, would you?' said Joanna in a voice like saccharin. 'You were dining in the isolated luxury of the Amber Palace. One of your regular haunts, is it?'

There was a pause in which Joanna could almost hear her heart beating. She did not care. He could be furious. The more he behaved badly towards her, the less the hurt.

She heard the short, deep chuckle. It was like a knife in her heart. It was a sound that twisted her emotions into string.

'So that's what's riling you, that I took Lucille to the Amber Palace?' The amusement seemed to go out of his voice. 'Now just you understand this, Joanna. I do exactly what I want to, when I want to. My actions are judged by no one except me, and definitely not by a young woman I've only known a couple of days.'

'I—I wasn't judging you,' Joanna trembled, seeking to find the right words. 'I was in no way criticising your right to do exactly as you please. I'm sorry if I gave that impression. As I told you before, I often say the wrong thing without meaning it.'

She sat there, plucking at the hem of the sheet, another shiny tear falling over her lower lashes and joining the one that glistened on her cheek. This conversation was becoming disastrous. She wished she was tucked up in bed, crying in privacy.

He leaned forward, seeing the hurt on her pale transparent face. He took the corner of the linen and dabbed at her cheeks, not very expertly, as if this was something quite new.

'Poor Joanna,' he said gently. 'Did it hurt that much? I'm sorry. Lucille found out that we had been to the Amber Palace last night and she was jealous. She asked me to take her. She is the wife of an old friend, and there was no reason to disappoint her. You may think she is very sophisticated and worldly, with two ex-husbands and a budding film career, but she doesn't have your youth, Joanna darling, and that makes her very vulnerable.'

'I'm vulnerable, too...' Joanna heard herself saying. 'It was my mistake ... last evening was ... so special.'

She found his arms coming round and under her, and he was lifting her out of her chair and onto his lap. The sudden closeness of his body took her breath away. He tilted her head back and his mouth found her lips, tasting their sweetness with a probing pressure that drained all her resistance. There was no mockery in him now, all was gentleness in his touch, and yet the arms round her were firm and unyielding. He was kissing her with an authority, demanding that she should respond with equal passion.

'Don't be afraid, darling Joanna,' he whispered, his fingers raking her hair as his mouth explored the hollows of her face. 'I won't force you. But you are so lovely. You can't know how soft your skin is...' He was untying the string that gathered the neck of her peasant blouse, pushing it from her shoulder with his face, his lips tracing the soft curves of her small breasts, heedless of the wisps of lace that separated them.

She felt the wild tingling sweeping through her body like a flame. Her hands were in the crisp dark hair of his head, but her mouth, so long starved of kisses, sought his, and they locked together in a kiss that was shattering in the strength of its passion. Their minds went swimming away into star-bursts of light, impossible sensations throbbing through their bodies.

Joanna knew that she could not stop him. If he carried her to the bed, it would happen. And she cared not. She was past thinking of her pride, of her resolutions of independence, nothing mattered now but this longing to be closer, to be so close that there was nothing between them except this magic of an Indian night.

'Darling … darling…' Joanna breathed, letting her breasts move against him, her long legs twisted round his knees.

His hands were hard and possessive on her waist, turning her so that he could lift her more easily. He was strong; he carried her like a child, negotiating the door and furniture with care, even though her arms were tightly round his neck and her kisses were painting his face with love.

It was like a tempest inside her, a fire coursing her veins; she was a dancer and her fingers were erotic, knowing without knowing, what was the right thing to do. She heard Matthew groaning as he laid her on the bed and his weight loomed over her, gentle yet heavy, encompassing her slighter frame, every inch of her from her toes to her face, swamped by this warm and glorious male body.

There was moonlight on the pale ceiling, that was all she saw. It was a sea of sensation, waves that rocked her higher and higher, a desperate longing that cut through all other thoughts and sent them tumbling into space … Matthew was crushing her with an intensity that made her want to cry out, the gentleness had gone, she could not breathe …

'Joanna. Joanna? Are you asleep? I'm back. Can I borrow some remover? I broke mine yesterday.'

Mandy's sharp young voice penetrated the room. She was calling from her bathroom across the hallway. At first Joanna did not even recognise the voice. She was lost somewhere on a plane that did not know anything but Matthew's kisses and his demanding body.

'Mandy ...? Mandy?' she said uncertainly, her voice sounding full of sleep.

'Sorry, if I woke you. I've broken my bottle of remover. Can I borrow yours? Is it in your bathroom? Can I go and get it?'

Matthew lay heavily against her, his face against the pillow. He did not move. She could feel his breath fanning her cheek.

'It's in the bathroom on the shelf,' said Joanna weakly, her arm flung across his back. 'Just take it. Take it.'

They heard Mandy go into the bathroom, banging the door noisily, humming a tune. 'Oh, I like your kind. Estee Lauder ... that's a posh make, isn't it? Mmn, nice.'

'Keep it,' Joanna offered almost weeping with disappointment as Matthew moved away from her very slightly. The spell was broken. The feelings were ebbing. All that glorious joy was vanishing somewhere ... why did it have to go ... where was it going ...? His face was glowing with sweat, long lines of shadow etching his proud features. He lifted himself onto one elbow and looked down at Joanna.

'What's the matter?' they heard Mandy

going on. She giggled. 'You sound funny. Have you got a man in there?'

She giggled again. It was obviously the last thing she expected of the strait-laced Miss Hamilton.

'Four,' said Joanna. 'Now, go away, and let me get some sleep.'

'Night-night. Pierre and I had a smashing time. I'll tell you about it tomorrow. I mean, in the morning.'

The door to Mandy's bedroom closed but she was still singing. Matthew eased himself off the bed. They both knew that they could not continue. Mandy had successfully brought everything back to normality. Joanna looked at her clothes, in wild disarray, and tried to cover herself.

Matthew rescued his jacket from somewhere on the floor, and bent down, kissing Joanna lightly on the forehead.

'Next time,' he said softly, his mouth against her ear, 'We'll make sure that Mandy is locked up.'

CHAPTER FIVE

It was the morning of the towers. They filmed three of Delhi's famous towers before packing to leave the Ashoka Hotel. The first was Qutb Minar, the seventh wonder of Hindustan, 234 feet of stone frills and balconies built in the 13th century.

'I'm not climbing up there,' said Mandy, not impressed by the fluted pink sandstone and grey granite walls. 'It's too high and it looks like a factory chimney.'

'You won't have to,' said Matthew. 'Unfortunately someone fell off in the crush and it's closed.'

'I can't even pronounce it,' she wailed, fanning herself with a large red straw hat she had bought in the hotel arcade. 'What a weird word.'

Near the unclimbable, unpronounceable Qutb Minar was another strange object; the Iron Pillar, a solid shaft of iron 24 feet high, inscribed with six lines of Sanskrit and not a speck of rust after 1,500 years out in the monsoon rains.

Joanna touched the pure cold iron with her fingertips. This one was a mystery. No one had any idea why the Hindu king, Chandra Varman, had the pillar built here in this courtyard, sometime in the 5th century. There was, however, a tremendous sense of the past and she dawdled, not wanting to leave.

The film crew were ahead; Andre with his heavy camera, Lucille with the clapperboard and Matthew's schedules; Pierre the most laden with boom microphone headphones and receiver slung in a satchel over his shoulder.

'Come along, Joanna. We haven't got all

day.'

Along the roadside were traces of the great battlements which had once been part of the vast fortress. It was easy to walk through Delhi's history, to explore and see the signs of decline and decay.

In the sad ruins of Ferozeshah Kotla, a fortress palace, stood the ancient Ashoka Pillar, which was already 1,500 years old when Firuz Shah decided to bring it to Delhi to grace his new palace.

'It took a special carriage with 42 wheels to move this pillar,' said Joanna, reading from her guide book. 'And to each wheel a rope was attached and 200 men pulled on each rope.'

'I can't see the point,' said Mandy, glancing up.

Everyone laughed and she could not understand why. Still she smiled as if she did. She was feeling happier today. Pierre was an excellent dancer, and he had promised to take her dancing again and she was already planning what to wear. It was such a pity he was foreign, and French at that. She preferred to think of him as an American, like Matthew.

Matthew said very little to Joanna. She was getting used to his absolute concentration when working. He had no time for small talk once he was filming, but she understood this now and did not mind. She had plenty of work of her own to do; her notebook was filling rapidly, page after page of shorthand and scrawled longhand. Now that she knew what she was doing, the ideas flowed effortlessly. Mandy's Diary was almost writing itself; her own much longer private notes needed far more thought.

Joanna was none too pleased to find that Mandy was hopeless at packing. The girl stood in the middle of a muddle of clothes and cosmetics, her cases overflowing with badly folded garments and piles of shoes. Joanna's own packing had taken ten minutes. She put the amber dress back into its gold and black box, wondering if she would have time to dispose of it. She was tempted to keep the dress.

She could not think of last night without a small smile touching her lips. She was not ashamed, but she was amazed at herself. That great flame of feeling had been new and shattering, and surprising. She had not known that such a wild and glorious passion lay hidden in the veins of her body. It was a long time since she had loved anyone. There had been no one since Bruce, and that had been such a young and innocent romance. They had been children playing at love, trusting in the future, not knowing that they did not have one.

'Oh Mandy...' said Joanna with some exasperation. 'Don't you know how to pack? We have to be out of the suite by mid-day.'

'My mum always does it for me,' said Mandy, attempting to fold one of her prize dresses.

'Let's start from the beginning,' said Joanna, emptying the cases onto the bed. There were shoes and bottles mixed up with fine fabrics. Joanna made no more comments. She was beginning to sound like a school mistress. Deftly she began to repack Mandy's belongings, hoping that Mandy was watching carefully. She did not want this performance again.

The delay meant that they missed the air conditioned express train on which they had reservations. Andre and Pierre had gone ahead in a taxi to the main railway station for the train to Agra. As they had the filming equipment with them, they boarded the train without the rest of the party.

Lucille was fuming by the time Joanna and Mandy emerged in the foyer with their luggage. Joanna tried to apologise without putting all the blame on Mandy. Matthew was none too pleased, but he was philosophical about it.

'We'll take the royal route,' he said. 'It's apparently a good road, and the scenery will be interesting.'

'It'll probably be quite fun,' said Joanna, determined to be cheerful at any cost. Mandy was looking sulky, knowing it was her fault; upset that Pierre had gone without her.

'Don't think I don't know why you've done this,' said Lucille as Matthew disappeared outside. 'It won't make any difference. He's not interested in you.'

Joanna caught her breath. The statement took her by surprise. 'Don't be ridiculous,' she said bluntly. 'I wouldn't deliberately miss a train for any reason. I'm afraid you've got your wires crossed, Lucille.'

'I know exactly what you are up to,' Lucille said, her face drawn into bitter accusation. 'Matthew Howard would be quite a catch for a foot-in-the-door reporter, but he's not available. Just you remember that.'

Joanna hesitated. She chose her words very carefully. She did not want to make an enemy of Lucille, or say anything that might get back to Matthew in a twisted form.

'Thank you for the advice, Lucille,' she said smoothly. 'But I'm sure we both know that Matthew does exactly what he wants to do. No one can manipulate him.'

The taxi was a battered 1970 Ambassador, the Indian people's one make of car.

They drove across the endless plain south-eastwards to Agra, the road lined with faded tombs and ruins, and small ragged villages.

The three on the back seat were hardly able to move on the smelly leather, the stink of petrol and oil in their nostrils. Matthew sat grimly in the middle so that Joanna and Mandy could at least get some relief from the open windows. It was a mistake to be travelling through the hottest part of the day, the

92

scorching wind off the plain soaring in temperature.

Majestic trees, planted for shade, gave brief protection as the taxi jolted and rumbled over pot holes and loose stones without losing speed. It seemed to Joanna that India was perpetually on the move, walking, cycling, by cart. There was a perpetual motion about the vast sub continent. An elephant was lifting great logs into a waiting lorry, his huge feet plodding slowly with enormous strength and dignity. His eyes followed the taxi, his trunk curled round the log like a cigar. He laboured unquestioningly, grey papery skin hanging in ancient folds.

'I wonder how old that elephant is,' said Mandy, hanging her head out of the window. 'Poor thing.'

Lucille looked into the driving mirror at the two young women in the back. They made her feel old and she did not like that. She was not used to roughing anything and the blanket of heat rising from the earth was turning the drive into a nightmare.

Joanna was also deep in thought, her face like a Madonna. She was appalled by the poverty of the little villages they drove through. Ragged children came begging to the car windows; groups of weary women washed piles of clothes at the village pump; the men gossiped in the shade. The hovels they lived in were hardly bigger than a kennel, many made from cakes of dung, and thatched with leaves. Dung was used for fuel and building, too valuable to simply dig back into the red earth.

'I'm going to be sick,' said Mandy in a small voice.

'Oh, hell,' said Lucille. 'Stop the car and let her get out.'

Matthew rapped on the driver's shoulder. 'Stop, please, at once.'

The driver brought the taxi to a screeching halt. He had the sense to roll into some shade. He immediately lit up a foul smelling cigarette, and stuck his elbow out of the window.

Joanna helped the half fainting girl out of the taxi. She put her arm round Mandy's waist, and took her out of sight behind some withered and stunted trees.

Mandy leaned weakly against the crusty bark. 'I'm so sorry,' she wept. 'I feel awful.'

'I'm not surprised,' said Joanna with feeling. 'It's a terrible journey. I should have insisted on waiting for the next train, even if it took days. That was the problem. There are so few express trains each day, you have to book in advance if you want a seat.' Joanna pushed some damp curls from the girl's neck.

She found a shady spot some further distance away, and persuaded Mandy to sit down. The colour was beginning to return to the girl's face.

'And to think it's probably pouring back home,' said Joanna, scanning the great

94

expanse of cloudless blue sky. 'It's very unfair. London would love a few days of this.'

'My mum gets arthritis in her knees. Sometimes she can hardly move. She's got a heat lamp. She'd like a bit of this sun.'

'We'll have to get you some travel pills when we get to Agra. Are you feeling better? I've some cologne pads in my handbag, and I'll fetch the iced water.'

Joanna made her way back across the dry, pitted red earth to the taxi where the others were slowly frying on the hot leather seats. Matthew had got out and was pacing the dusty path.

'Is Mandy all right?' he asked.

'Recovering.'

'I've a flask of brandy. Would she drink some?'

'Yes, that would settle her stomach. I'll take the iced water too. She is feeling better.'

'I hope this is not going to take all day,' Lucille grumbled. 'I'm melting away and my dress is creased to high heaven. At least there's a breeze when we're moving.'

Mandy was not averse to sipping the brandy. It was a good cognac and the liquid ran like fire down her throat, burning and soothing at the same time. Joanna bathed her face with the cold water. Somewhere far off came the tinkle of buffalo bells and the creaking of a laden cart. Overhead a single plane droned. The heat haze was solid.

'We'll fly back, I promise,' said Joanna. 'Even if I have to pay for it myself.'

Spots of bright light dazzled her eyes. The sun picked on any smooth surface and set it into bursts of sparklers ... a piece of broken glass, her watch face, a can, a glint of granite in a stone.

'We can't stay here all day. You'd better sit in the front, where there's more breeze. If we can get Lucille to move.'

The driver had dozed off across the wheel, his lank hair glistening with oil, running into his stained collar. Mandy shook her head; she'd rather stay in the back.

A cart rumbled by drawn by a pair of heavy sweating buffalo. Their driver was stretched out across some sacks, a cloth over his face, asleep; the buffalo obviously knew the way.

Matthew was reading the torn advertisements on the flaking plaster of a shrine. There was also a stone kos minar, a distance marker, so tall it looked like a monument itself.

The drive continued. They drove over beautifully arched stone bridges, some built more than 400 years before but still in use; the river beds beneath dry and cracked.

Along the roadside men were sitting on the ground, cutting up cow-hide and making sandals. They were no longer the Untouchables and stared at the European faces with curiosity.

Joanna was well aware that she was sitting close to Matthew, their bare arms touching and sticking as the taxi thundered over the uneven road, but there was no pleasure in it. The discomfort was too much for any thoughts except how soon would they reach Agra.

After one crater-like rut that sent everyone shooting towards the roof of the vehicle, Matthew took Joanna's hand. She was too hot and sticky to want him to hold it and she tried to withdraw from his grasp.

'I will try to make up for this,' he said. 'I could not be more sorry.'

'It's not your fault,' Joanna murmured. They were coming to the shabby outskirts of a town. It could be Agra.

Suddenly they saw it ... the fabulous dome of the Taj Mahal, towering over the low flat roofed buildings that formed the horizon. Joanna's spirits soared. Even Mandy looked interested.

The taxi began nosing its way through the crooked roads and narrow lanes, thronged with jostling people. They passed the grim and foreboding Red Fort of Agra, so different from the pearly washed marble of the Taj Mahal. Their driver did not seem to know where their hotel was. Joanna felt they would be well rid of him. He was the least helpful person they had come across.

A young boy in white trousers and shirt, astride a bicycle, directed the now sullen driver to the Clark's Shiraz. He probably works there, thought Joanna, as the boy grinned at them.

Joanna, breathed a sigh of relief as the taxi swung into the drive of the Clark's Shiraz and drew up outside an impressive and re-assuringly modern hotel. A large fountain played in front of the canopied entrance. A turbaned doorman leaped forward to open the door of the battered taxi. Flowers grew in profusion in the garden, but no one lingered. They could only think of getting to the bar and ordering iced cokes.

The taxi driver, as well as being a bad driver, was also a rogue. He tried to insist on double the price Matthew had agreed with him in Delhi. A crowd of workmen and gardeners gathered for the argument, joining in with their opinions.

'Price agreed in Delhi, sahib, was drive to Agra,' ventured an older workman. 'Price now asking is also for drive back to Delhi.'

'But I don't want to go back to Delhi,' Matthew exploded.

The old man opened his hands in resignation.

'Driver does, sahib,' he said.

The driver was putting on a great act, wailing and wringing his hands, pouring out his story of hardship to an appreciative audience. It was an old trick.

Matthew came striding into the bar where

Joanna had set up iced drinks for everyone. Pierre and Andre had already arrived and were being teased for travelling the easy way.

'Did you pay him?' asked Lucille. 'I hope you didn't tip the crook.'

'It's no hardship for me to pay,' said Matthew, after a long drink. He had not touched the iced drink in the thermos, leaving it all for the three women. 'But I do not like being tricked. It was a real con. I ought to have called the police, but what would have been the use?'

'What did you do?' Joanna was curious. Matthew was so rich, and the driver a pathetic creature.

'I paid up. But I gave him the agreed fare in rupees, and the rest in English pound notes. He can't take them to a bank because of their currency restrictions. He'll have to change them on street corners. He won't lose on them, but it'll take time and trouble and he might get caught.'

His dark eyes suddenly locked with Joanna's, as if the others did not exist. He bent towards her a little mockingly.

'Do you approve?' he asked, taking her glass from her hand and finishing it for her. It was a gesture of intimacy that did not escape Lucille.

'If you drink so fast, you'll be ill,' said Joanna mildly.

'I am never ill,' he said, nodding to the barman for two more cokes.

'I'm sorry you have been travel sick,' said Pierre to Mandy. 'Perhaps you would like to rest for the evening?'

'No, I wouldn't,' Mandy said firmly. 'I feel quite all right now.'

Mandy took the key of their suite and went upstairs for a shower and to change. There were flowers and fruit in their rooms, and from the wide panoramic windows a view of the distant Taj, white and ethereal above the tree-tops. Just when she was beginning to get used to Delhi, Joanna whisked her off to somewhere new. Had there been a cash prize? She wished she had taken it. Where was the glamour and fame in all this dust and heat? When the documentary eventually got shown on the box, her friends would go out or switch to the other channel.

'What have I said wrong?' Pierre turned to Joanna, crest-fallen. 'Is she angry with me?'

'Don't worry. She doesn't like being bossed around. She is simply showing a small spark of independence. You'll see her later.'

The group dissolved to their rooms. Joanna was disappointed and dismayed that Matthew had not spoken to her about last night, and apart from that brief moment when he took her hand, it might not have happened at all.

She should have known that it meant nothing to Matthew, merely a pleasant sexual encounter with someone a little different from the run of Hollywood starlets. Perhaps her coolness and remoteness had been a challenge to his masculinity. It was too late to wish it had never happened, and Joanna was honest enough to admit that she had not exactly been screaming for help.

Mandy was sitting on the edge of the bath wrapped in a big towel, shivering, her wet hair dripping down her back.

'I've forgotten my hair dryer,' she moaned. 'I left it behind at the Ashoka Hotel. Do you think they'll forward it?'

'Oh dear ... I doubt it, and anyway it would never reach Agra in time. I'll see what I can do. In the meantime you can borrow mine.'

Across the fringe of trees, about a mile away, Joanna saw the dazzling pearly dome of the Taj Mahal and the slender spires of the four Minarets. How beautiful, she thought, more calmly. How Bruce would have loved this view.

The hotel had been built in the former residential area of the colonial settlers, in the garden of what had once been a prosperous house. Now these low, rambling colonnaded homes were in ruins, boarded up with planks and shuttered with sacks. Some had been taken over by squatter families, others were deserted, decaying into the brown wilderness of the neglected gardens. It was a sad reminder of the long gone Victorian era when Englishwomen came to live in India and imprinted their customs and values on the land.

The five floors of the Clark's Shiraz

dominated the immediate sky-line, yet faded into insignificance when compared with the great mausoleum.

Joanna showered quickly and changed into a thin blue flounced check skirt and toning silk blouse, then hurried out into the warm corridor, and walked down the wide staircase. The enormous picture windows gave a panoramic view of the plain as she descended.

The Taj drew her like a magnet. Now that she was here, it was impossible to wait, so near and yet not there until the morning. She could almost imagine the soft white arms of the Lady of the Taj welcoming her, beckoning ... She had to go now and feast her eyes, refresh her soul, to pay a small homage to the greatest symbol of married love.

'How far is the Taj Mahal from here?' Joanna asked at the reception desk.

'About a mile,' the Indian girl answered with a charming smile. She was very beautiful with gold studs in her ears and a red paste caste mark on her forehead. 'Shall I order a taxi for you?'

Joanna smiled and shook her head. 'No, thank you. I can walk a mile. It's cooler now.'

'Turn left at the hotel gates and then it is straight on, across one round-about and one cross-roads. You cannot lose your way because you can always see the Taj from wherever you are in Agra.'

As Joanna stepped out into the sunshine of

the late afternoon, a score of rickshaw boys, thin and brown in tattered clothes, pulled their cumbersome bicycle rickshaws forward.

They surged towards their prey. 'No, thank you,' said Joanna, shaking her head. 'No, thank you. I want to walk.'

They did not believe her, persistently following her down the road. A memsahib who wanted to walk ... amazing. She stepped out briskly, wanting to rid herself of this embarrassing entourage. Gradually the boys gave up until two were left. One was a stunted little lad of about fourteen, with a drab and rusty bicycle, the leather seat split in several places. The other boy was a taller, handsome brown youth with gleaming white teeth and flashing eyes and a reasonably clean shirt. His bicycle was shining and decorated with gaudy tassels, and his rickshaw had a smart blue canopy fringed with bright red silk.

'Missy have ride. Sun too hot. Missy not walk,' said the youth, slowly pedalling behind her, his wheels creaking in time.

'Please go away. I really do want to walk.'

'Missy soon very tired. I take to Taj.'

Joanna did not answer. It seemed hopeless to argue.

'Very cheap.'

'Not today, thank you. Tomorrow perhaps.'

'Yes, tomorrow, what time?' the youth asked quickly. Joanna couldn't help laughing. She wondered if he had an appointments system. 'After breakfast sometime.'

'Eight o'clock?'

'Perhaps nine...'

'Eight cool. Nine hot,' said the young man bossily.

'I do not know yet,' said Joanna firmly. 'I'll see.'

The youth wheeled round in mid road, standing upright on the pedals and left with a gay salute. 'I will wait,' he called out cheerfully.

The ragged boy was still following her. 'Missy have free ride,' he whined in a voice peculiarly hoarse for one so young. He saw the doubt in Joanna's eyes and thought she was dubious about his ability. He pushed up his torn shirt sleeve. 'Me very stong,' he said, flexing non-existent muscles.

His elbows and knees were just bones poking against dingy skin. He was very thin, with stained teeth and yellowed eyes.

'Free ride,' he offered again, jauntily.

'All right,' said Joanna. She had not the heart to resist. She knew her free ride would cost her a substantial tip, but it seemed important to allow him the dignity of being generous when he had so little to give. The boy grinned, helped her up the single steep step and then swung himself up into the high saddle. They went off at a great rate, bumping and swaying all over the uneven road.

When Joanna got used to the jolting pace and discovered the safest way to sit without sliding off the narrow leather seat, she began to enjoy the ride. This was the way to travel. The pace gave her time to enjoy the gardens and parkland as they passed, to look at ruined houses behind rusty gates, to see a buffalo dragging a grass cutting machine.

She alighted at the entrance to the Taj Gardens with a sense of awe. This was a dream coming true. But outside on the burnt grass were stalls selling bangles, sweetmeats, crude souvenirs and postcards. Joanna found them jarring.

Joanna gave the lad some rupees and he seemed pleased. He pocketed it quickly. 'I'll wait,' he said.

'I have no idea how long I shall be,' she warned.

He shrugged, stuck something into his mouth and began to chew. 'Okay,' he said.

She went through the archway of the entrance gate into the coolness of the inner chamber with its high vaulted roof. Moving out onto the steps that led down into the gardens, not really prepared for what she would see.

She stopped and held her breath, completely taken aback by the enchanting loveliness which lay before her at the end of an avenue of cypress trees, coolly reflected in the shallow watercourse, its marble beauty soaring towards the sky.

No photograph or painting could capture its

105

magic. It was like a fantastic mirage, shimmering in the heat haze. Joanna stepped aside to allow people to pass, never taking her eyes off the Taj, wanting this first impression imprinted indelibly on her memory.

'I never thought it would be like this,' she said aloud. 'I never dreamed it could be so perfect.'

'Nor I,' said Matthew.

She was not surprised to see him. He would have had the same feeling of impatience once they were so near.

She was extraordinarily happy that he should be there beside her, and yet at the same time she wanted to be alone. He knew what she was feeling and gave her the briefest of smiles.

'We will go back together,' he said, strolling away from her. 'Do not leave without me.'

Joanna felt a weakness sweeping through her. His tall figure had the power to stir her emotions, and she knew she was becoming hopelessly encircled by a mesh of feelings over which she seemed to have no control. Whatever she did, she was going to be the loser. No man like Matthew would ever stay in her life. She was no more than an interlude ... a novelty.

Joanna went down the steps to the marble path beside the long and still watercourse, putting her sad thoughts away as she began the long, long walk towards the Taj. It was like walking along some endless aisle in a green and

106

roofless church; there was little sound beyond the twitterings of brilliantly-hued birds darting among the trees; the atmosphere was one of peace and reverence and great love.

She felt as if she had been there before, that she knew the woman who was buried, the little Mumtaz Mahal, whom the Shah loved so much that when she died in childbirth, his hair turned grey. So few people's lives were enriched by such glorious love. They were the favoured few. To taste such love, even for a short time, was surely better than never at all ...

As Joanna neared the mausoleum, she was glad that Matthew had gone ahead. She felt a great wonder at a building of such beauty, and yet was acutely aware that she was treading in the footsteps of the grief-stricken Shah Jahan. How many times had he stood in the gardens watching his army of builders, carving and chipping and heaving the huge blocks of marble?

Rows of sandals had been left at the double flight of steps up to the marble platform which supported the Taj. Their owners walked barefoot over the marble flagstones, entering the building between exquisite trellis screens carved from solid marble. All could come, even the poorest ... no one was ever turned away, especially on Fridays when entrance was free and the crowds came.

An attendant tied felt over-shoes over her

feet though Joanna was prepared to go barefoot. She saw a pair of expensive shoes, large, hand-sewn supple brown leather shoes from Jermyn Street, London. They must belong to Matthew. It was touching that he had taken off his shoes and was walking barefoot like an Indian.

The Taj was so much larger than she had expected; postcards and calendars gave no sense of its size. The dome itself was mounted on a drum, its golden crest pointing to heaven; beyond was the slow river; the same river that flowed through Delhi.

Light filtered into the main chamber from the smaller domes, shafts of glowing sunlight, glinting on the inlaid precious stones. The tomb of Mumtaz Mahal, the Moghul queen, lay in the centre chamber under the huge vaulted dome, a marble sky. A few inches away was the larger tomb of her husband, Shah Jahan, making it strangely crowded yet right that the two lovers should be together.

The walls and the tombs were intricately inlaid with flowers and leaves of precious gems and stones, cornelian, onyx, agate, chrysolite, jade, gold and silver ... so evenly laid that Joanna's skimming fingers could feel no edge.

A few sprays of fresh jasmine lay on the queen's tomb, a small offering of love, the fragrant scent mingling with the musk and incense.

She went down the worn and ancient steps

burrowing steeply into the crypt directly below the tombs, where the bodies lay at peace. She ducked her head to miss an overhanging ledge. A strange musty smell, centuries old, invaded everywhere, and in the lamp lit dimness Joanna felt intensely moved. Dust and ashes, never. The devoted lovers were somewhere still.

'I don't like being reminded of the permanence of death,' said Matthew who was standing there. 'I have far too much to do. Let's go back into the sunlight. We have paid our respects.'

He was ready now for company, and so was Joanna. They went through the bays and archways of shimmering light, out into the warmth. The continual stream of pilgrims were still treading the long walk by the watercourse, the colours of saris like many butterflies seeking the heart of the flower. The sun was going down and the building was now a pearly pink, bathed in the last glowing rays.

'People are so quiet,' said Joanna. 'There are no raised voices. Imagine the noise if this were in London.'

'Or New York,' said Matthew. 'The noisiest city in the world.'

They sat on the carefully mown and watered grass under weeping trees. The grass was so green compared to the burnt brown stubble outside the gardens. Other groups of families and friends sat about, quiet, letting the restfulness of the garden and the tranquillity of the Taj restore some of the damage of life.

'I will never be able to write about this,' said Joanna. 'It's quite beyond my ability. I can see it all, even feel deeply, but I will never be able to find the right words. Perhaps they don't exist.'

'You'll be in good company. Even the best writers have failed when it comes to the Taj. Just write from the heart and some of it will come through.'

'It's easy for you, with a camera. You just point and press a button, and hey presto ... there it is.'

'Very simple,' Matthew agreed. He was stretched out beside her, resting on his elbows, his face more relaxed, even younger looking. A lazy gleam came into his dark eyes. 'You are looking at me so intently, Joanna darling. Shall I send you a photograph when I get back to LA? So that you won't forget me.'

'No thank you,' said Joanna primly. She did not want to be reminded that he would be returning to America soon. Nor did she need a photograph. His face was indelibly printed on her mind.

'Are you thinking that I am very callous?' he went on, reaching for her hand. He turned it over, studying the palm and the map of her life. 'Last night I made love to you, and today you have been ignored. Most women would be furious. And rightly so. It's insufferable behaviour.'

'It didn't bother me,' said Joanna lightly.

'Liar. The hurt is in your eyes. Do you want to know why I have been so cruel to you?' His voice was not mocking now. It was serious, and now that he was not towering over her, he looked more vulnerable.

'If you like,' she shrugged.

'You see before you six foot two inches of confused male,' he confided. 'I want to make love to you, very much . . . oh Joanna, you have no idea how that cool and remote image of yours is a challenge to me. It puts wicked thoughts into my head. But something is making me stop. And I don't know why. Can it be that I am falling in love with you?'

'Then don't,' said Joanna, forcing the tremor out of her voice. 'I don't want you to be in love with me. It would be disastrous.'

'I agree,' he said. 'I am the last person on earth who should fall in love. I'm selfish, arrogant, egotistical. Any woman I loved would suffer. She would never know if I were hers. She could never be sure.'

Joanna wanted to cry out that she didn't care, that she would accept life with him on any terms, that she would follow him to the moon. But she said none of these things.

'I think it would be best if we both forgot about last night; put it down to the heat, the romantic music and the erotic dancing.'

'How very sensible,' Matthew agreed.

'After all, we are both here to work,' she pointed out. 'Not for a romantic dalliance.'

111

'No dallying,' he said.

She had an idea he was laughing at her, but he had turned his face away and she could not see. She heard the pattering of a chipmunk's paws as it scuttled along a path, the soft murmur of water, the evening song of birds.

He pointed to a tiny groove which crossed the heart line on her palm. His head was close to hers, lips near enough to touch.

'See that little line,' he said, tracing it with his finger. 'That's me. That's your romantic dalliance in an Indian hotel bedroom.'

'Really? Insignificant, isn't it?' She was surprised that she had managed to say something quite cutting. He dropped her hand and rose to his feet. He did not help her up.

'It's time we got back to the others,' he said.

They went back in separate rickshaws. The lad was still waiting for Joanna, and his face lit up when she re-appeared. She was in no mood to walk now and was glad of the uphill ride.

She knew the conversation could have gone quite differently. She had deliberately defused the situation. But why? They could have been returning now, together, their arms entwined or hands linked, enjoying the beginning of a love affair …

Instead they sat at dinner like strangers, as if their arms had never been round each other, as if their lips had never touched. It was unreal; now they were characters in a play with lines to speak. Had Matthew really said he had been falling in love with her? He gave little sign of it, paying attention to Lucille and making a lot of technical conversation which Joanna could not follow.

Joanna made her excuses early and went up to her room. She had work to do. It took her a long time. The Taj had affected her deeply and it was not easy to write her notes. Its beauty defeated her, and she turned to Mandy's Diary which was less demanding.

She lay in bed unable to sleep, all her thoughts turning in her mind. It was so unlike Joanna. She usually slept well and effortlessly. Now she moved about the bed, alternately chilled by the air conditioning, then too hot from the Indian night. She did not know how long she lay waiting for sleep, anxious now because she had a busy day ahead and needed to be fresh.

There was a discreet knock at her door. Joanna looked at her watch. It was only just after midnight. She pulled on a wrap, wondering if Mandy was ill or wanted something.

It was Matthew, a suede jacket over his open necked shirt. He took in her nightie and wrap in some surprise, but did not comment.

'Get dressed, Joanna. We're going out,' he ordered her.

'I beg your pardon. I'm trying to get some sleep.'

'What a ridiculously old-fashioned notion,

going to bed so early. Is it an English custom? I'll give you three minutes to put something decent on.'

Joanna was too tired for games. She sighed and tried to close the door, but Matthew was firmly in the way. He looked very tall and dark in the doorway and she could not see the expression on his face. No doubt it was one of amusement.

'Please go away.'

'We are going to see the Taj Mahal.'

'I've seen the Taj Mahal.' She was trying to sound crushing, but it did not work.

'We are going to see it by moonlight. I have ordered a rickshaw. The boy is waiting outside. Put some clothes on, and we can go.'

Joanna wearily pushed some hair out of her eyes. He was back on form, telling her what to do as if she were a child.

'Seeing the Taj by moonlight is something really special,' she said. 'I know that. You either go alone, or you go with someone special, the kind of sensitive person who wouldn't spoil the magic. You don't come into that category.'

She shut the door firmly and leaned against it. He would not ask her again.

CHAPTER SIX

'Hey, shake a leg, sleepy-head. Wake up. Let's see this old Taj before it gets too hot.'

Mandy was shaking Joanna's bare shoulder, her pert young face full of good humour for once. She had already had a swim in the hotel pool with Pierre, and his open admiration for her slim figure and mini-bikini had been very encouraging.

A tray of tea was at her bedside, and the usual bowl of delicious fruit. The brilliant blue sky told her it was still India, with its bewitching charm, scorched red-brown earth and insufferable heat. She remembered Matthew's midnight call and her happiness ebbed away. He was not the kind of man to risk another rebuff.

'I've been swimming with Pierre,' said Mandy, sitting on the side of the bed and helping herself to a banana.

'He's not part of the prize,' said Joanna mischievously.

'I wish he was,' said Mandy. 'He's absolutely fabulous. He likes me, too. The attraction is mutual,' she added quickly as though expecting Joanna to deny it.

'I'm sure it is, but don't forget we go home soon. I don't want you to go home with a broken heart.'

'Not me,' said Mandy cheerfully. 'But it doesn't have to end. I've got plans.'

The serving of breakfast was nearly over by the time they got down to the dining room. Andre and Pierre rose and said 'Good-morning.' Lucille had been to the hotel's hairdressing salon already and was looking very smart. Matthew had eaten and left.

Joanna's apprehension increased. She remembered Matthew's closeness and his arms gripping her, how her own dormant senses had suddenly come alive to meet the urgency of his mouth ... If only she could just surrender, give in to that overpowering attraction. All the empty years had been such a waste of being young, alive and with love to give. She had been waiting, waiting for someone special, and she knew Matthew was special ... strong, arrogant and yet still sensitive and funny.

But she was nothing to him, just a little fun while on location. He did not want a commitment or to be tied. He was a free man. She drew her pride round her like a protective cloak and prepared to be hurt.

'Fruit juice,' she ordered over-loudly to the hovering steward. 'And scrambled eggs please.'

The menu card was a blur in her hands. She could feel herself shaking. She must be losing her senses. Her cheeks flamed. She must pull herself together.

The steward brought coffee, juice, iced water

116

and a small package. It bore the name of one of the curio shops in the hotel foyer. She opened it slowly, knowing without seeing, that it was going to tear her to shreds. Inside was an ivory box, exquisitely carved with skeins of wild geese flying over painted storks, egrets and flamingos.

Joanna lifted the lid. Nestling on a velvet cushion was a ring, an antique Indian ring with a red-winking blood ruby set in intricately wrought gold. It was heavy and very old.

Mandy gasped. 'Joanna. How marvellous. Is it a present? Who's it from?'

'I don't know,' said Joanna, unfolding a note.

'I will understand if you don't speak to me this morning,' he had written. 'But don't send this back. It once belonged to a princess. Just give me a smile and I'll be happy.'

'You have an unknown admirer,' said Mandy excitedly, slicing the top off her boiled egg. 'What fun. Who is it?'

'It's a joke,' said Joanna, calmly refolding the note. 'I shall return it, of course. I can't keep such an expensive present.'

'Why not? I would,' said Mandy, her eyes devouring the glowing ruby. 'It looks so old. It probably belonged to some beautiful Indian princess at the Moghul Court. I expect her lover had it made especially for her.'

Joanna's fingers were exploring the intricate setting like a blind person. Perhaps it had even

117

belonged to the Lady of the Taj herself. The Shah had loved her and given her many jewels. Where had they all gone? Some must have survived the centuries.

She hated Matthew for giving her such a perfect present. He had known it was exactly the kind of beautiful box that would appeal to her, even without the jewel inside. It was easy for him to throw around his money. A cheque here, a diner's card there. It was becoming a game for him ... how many throws of the dice before jack-pot, before the aloof Miss Hamilton fell into his bed?

None, thought Joanna decisively, re-wrapping the gift. It was forfeit time. He had over-thrown his luck.

The handsome, clean-shirted rickshaw boy was waiting for them at the gates of the hotel. He ran forward, grinning and good-humoured, the tassels on the canopy swinging, the leather seat obviously dusted for the occasion. His eyes lit up when he saw Mandy with her bobbing fair curls and scarlet knickerbockers and lacy jump sweater.

Mandy blossomed under the boy's admiring glances. Joanna arranged to follow them in another rickshaw, drawn by the thin ragged lad of yesterday.

'Bansi. My name Bansi,' he said eagerly. 'I take you again, memsahib? Free ride.'

'Not a free ride,' said Joanna, climbing aboard. 'I'll pay the proper fare. You'll never

118

make any money giving free rides.'

'Okay,' he said, chewing and spitting, his face wreathed in grins.

For once Mandy reacted when they reached the gardens of the Taj Mahal. She was overwhelmed by the mausoleum, wandering around in a kind of daze unaware that Andre and Pierre were close by recording her every expression, every word.

'This is certainly a groovy kind of place. He must have been real gone on her,' she said. 'But I still reckon it's a goofy idea. Building a great place like this just for a dead woman.'

She turned to Pierre for his opinion. The handsome young man's face was gentle, as if explaining something to a child.

'But yes, she was some woman,' he said, removing his head-phones. 'And their love, it was something special. Only a few people experience this kind of love.'

'Oh rubbish,' said Mandy with a giggle, embarrassed. 'I don't believe you.'

'Perhaps you will be one of those lucky ones. This kind of special love for another person is like a thunderbolt from the sky,' said Pierre. 'You know if it has hit you. Sometimes it lasts together for a lifetime, then you are very lucky indeed. For others it can be for a day, perhaps a few hours ... but nothing is ever quite the same again. Nothing ever comes up to those moments.'

Joanna knew that Matthew was looking at

her, his dark eyes quite unreadable and fathomless; she did not dare to look back at him. Lucille was repairing her face in a mirror, but in it she could see Matthew's reflection. Andre was staring at the ground as if his past lay in the closely cropped velvet green grass.

'I'll let you know if I get hit by a thunderbolt,' said Mandy, breaking the silence. She smiled at Pierre and for a moment her European prettiness held all the delicate beauty of an Indian woman. The shade of the cypress tree deepened her light tan, and in the shadows of her face was all mystery. The fair hair became a freak of the sunshine. Suddenly her eyes were very deep and veiled in secret knowledge.

'Help,' she said in a small voice. 'I think I'm being hit.'

Joanna moved away, across the lawn. She could not bear to stay with the two young people. How could there be so much sky ... it went on forever, stretching past blue horizons into other hemispheres.

Not a leaf stirred. A gold crested bird hopped down and pecked at the dust near her feet, quite unafraid. A grey chipmunk scuttled across the path and up a tree, disappearing into the foliage. The gardens were alive with small animals.

Joanna felt so restless that her writing mind would not function. She could not settle to anything, neither notes or thoughts.

'Come to a creative blank?' asked Matthew intuitively. 'I know the feeling. It's all so perfect, there's very little one can add.'

She nodded. He had a way of coming up on her without her seeing. It was a little unnerving.

'Of course, as you said, I have only to point the camera and press a button, so my problems are minimal,' he added drily.

'I was joking,' said Joanna. 'I do realise that there is far more to your work than merely pointing the camera. I have seen *Planet Eleven*.'

'Have you?' He sounded pleased. 'I thought you hadn't seen it.'

'I never said that I had seen it, or that I hadn't seen it,' said Joanna, being deliberately awkward.

'I was just about to have a copy flown out and give a private showing. Mandy might like an evening at the flicks.'

'Don't let me stop you then. I'm sure she would be thrilled by the compliment. Anyway, it is a film that bears being seen again.'

He stood in front of her, his height almost threatening, his shirt open at the neck.

'How many times have you seen my film?' he asked. 'Come on, tell the truth. No hedging, Miss Hamilton.'

She could smell the stinging fragrance of his aftershave, and the warm masculine scent of his body. A strange sensation of fire ran through her limbs, making her skin tingle. She could not remember what he had just said. That mocking smile, those curved lips, his closeness, had wiped every word from her memory. She longed to pull his head down to her, to feel again the hardness of his mouth against hers. She was both confused and elated.

'Confess now.' he repeated. 'How many times have you seen *Planet Eleven*? Don't try to deny it. Remember I can read your eyes.'

Joanna immediately dropped her gaze, her lashes sweeping over the truth she hoped Matthew had not noticed. She had no wish for him to know how much he still affected her.

'Twice,' she said. 'It's a good film.' She was telling the truth. It was an extraordinary film. 'I shan't mind seeing it again.'

'I'll wire the States then. They'll fly it out. We might have it by tomorrow night, with any luck.'

'We shall have moved on by then,' said Joanna, glad to return to a business-like tone of conversation. 'There's still the ghost city at Fatehpur Sikri to see and Udaipur, the Venice of the East.'

'Do you think Mandy will survive any more ruins and temples?' he grinned.

'As long as the handsome Pierre continues to hold her hand, I'm sure Mandy will look at anything,' said Joanna.

'And who is going to hold your hand?' he

demanded, almost harshly.

'No one need hold my hand,' she said briskly. 'I like being in India and I like what I'm doing. No one is required to feel protective or supportive. I've looked after myself for seven years and barring accidents will continue to do so.'

'Would you consider meeting me as an accident?'

'No, I would rate it as merely incidental. By the way, I am returning your gift. I'll have it sent to your room.' Joanna heaved a sigh of relief. She had been rehearsing the words for hours, but now they were out. Matthew did not look particularly dismayed.

'No need to do that. I don't want it. Send it to a jumble sale, put it in the bin, chuck it out of a window. Do exactly what you like; it really doesn't bother me.'

Joanna was shocked at his callousness about such a beautiful and valuable object. If that was what he thought of the ring and the ivory box, then in his eyes it was a gift of little value. She was glad that she had decided not to keep it.

'Right,' she said, turning on her heel.

'Hang on a minute. Don't be in such a hurry. I want to talk to you.' Joanna hurried towards the film crew hoping to reach them before the conversation became personal.

'There's nothing to talk about unless it's the trip,' she said. 'I'm sure all the arrangements are satisfactory. Mr Wilberforce is pleased with Mandy's Diary, and I have no more worries.'

'So everything's just dandy,' he snapped.

'Just dandy,' she said, tossing her head.

It was a gruelling morning as the sun rose higher. Everyone began to wilt. Mandy and Pierre were stretched out in the shade of the cypress trees; Lucille was fanning herself with her large brimmed white straw hat; Andre was sitting in some shade, mopping his forehead with a handkerchief. Only Matthew was still wandering about, looking for new angles, new shots, his imagination still frantically working.

Joanna was wilting too. The loss of sleep was beginning to tell and she dozed in the sunshine, seeing the fringe of her own lashes against the sun. It was so quiet, with only the bird's song, and the murmur of water and low, hushed voices of the lilting Indian dialects.

She was suffering and it wasn't fair. He had everything, looks, money, success. Why couldn't he have left her alone? She wanted to return to London, to her career, in one piece, not a splintered personality with her silly heart yearning for a man who would not give her a moment's thought.

'Move,' he commanded from above. 'You'll burn if you don't take care. And you should never go to sleep in the sun.'

'Who woke me up?' she retorted. 'I didn't ask you to come banging on my door at midnight.'

'You don't know what you missed.'

'I know what I missed ... a good night's sleep. You really have no consideration for anyone.'

Suddenly Matthew grasped her arm and his eyes bored into hers. 'Look, what's with you this morning? You've done nothing but snap at me. I thought all English women had charming manners and pleasant natures.'

Joanna was saved having to think of a suitably cutting reply by the arrival of Mandy and Pierre. Pierre ambled over, his white cotton shirt sticking to his shoulder blades.

'I think we've all had enough,' he said to Matthew.

'Right,' said Matthew, getting up from the grass. 'We've done well. There's some good shots in the bag. Back to the hotel, folks— lunch and a siesta.'

'Coming swimming?' Mandy invited Pierre with a smile.

'A moment ago you were exhausted,' he teased.

'I recover very quickly,' said Mandy, tucking her arm through his.

Lucille sighed deeply and began to collect the clapperboard and her belongings from the grass. 'I thought she would say that.' In the heat, the carefully applied eyeliner had streaked into the fine creases of the thin skin round her eyes.

Joanna had left the ivory box and the ring in the hotel safe. Supposing she gave them to Bansi, the little lad who was straining every muscle to pedal her up the slow gradient to the Clark's Shiraz? But she had doubts. Would he be able to keep the proceeds? Perhaps he might even be accused of stealing the items, with no one believing that a white memsahib would give him such gifts. No, that was not the way to help Bansi.

Then the answer came. Who had been devouring the ruby ring with covetous eyes? Mandy ... she would be delighted to have them. They could be a special souvenir of her prize trip.

Mandy and Pierre went swimming. Joanna felt a pang of envy at their carefree enjoyment of each other's company, so uncomplicated and wholesome. Wholesome was not normally a word that was applied to falling in love, but the two young people were like puppies, romping and playing, taking pleasure from each other's uncommitted admiration.

As Joanna showered, there came a knock at the door. Exasperated she wrapped a big towel round her, and went wet-footed to see who it was. She hoped it was not Matthew. She opened the door a crack.

'Hello?'

It was Lucille. She had made a quick change into a sleek sun-dress which showed off her Californian-tanned shoulders and shrieked

Fifth Avenue.

'May I come in?' asked the older woman.

'I'm having a shower,' said Joanna.

'I won't be a minute, but I have something to say to you.' Lucille said it in a way that warned she would not go away until she had. Joanna opened the door reluctantly.

Lucille immediately sat herself in an armchair, crossing her legs, swinging her high-arched foot. She was wearing the kind of Italian sandals, so narrow and strappy that they were held together by a feat of engineering, that would have cost Joanna a week's salary.

'What could you possibly want to say to me?' Joanna said casually.

'I believe you have something that really belongs to me,' said Lucille, coming straight to the point. 'How you got hold of them, I don't know. I won't inquire. But I want them back.'

'I've got something of yours?' Joanna repeated slowly. She ignored the tone of accusation in Lucille's voice. 'I really don't know what you're talking about.'

'I understand from the jeweller's shop in the foyer that Matthew purchased some gifts for me. They were supposed to be delivered to me this morning, after he'd left the hotel. He knows I don't get up too early. But Mandy tells me you have them ... the ruby and the ivory box? They were meant for me, and I'd like them.'

Joanna felt the blood drain from her face. The chilly air-conditioning of the room accentuated the coldness that crept round her heart. The gifts had not been from Matthew as an apology, as a temptation, as a compliment ... they had not been meant for her at all. They were for Lucille. She felt a rush of shame as she recalled her high-handed conversation with him in the Taj gardens. He must have thought she was out of her mind. Then she realised Matthew had thought they were discussing the amber dress which he had sent her in Delhi.

Joanna pretended to towel her tumble of chestnut hair, taking some satisfaction from the fact that her hair looked good even wet.

'Oh so that solves the mystery,' she said lightly. 'I've been wondering who sent them. I put them in the hotel safe though I had no idea whether they were of any value or not. They could be just replicas.'

'Matthew doesn't buy replicas,' said Lucille.

'The steward gave me the package at breakfast. Didn't Mandy tell you that also? There was no name on the package. And we were also very late down for breakfast, so perhaps that also added to the confusion. However, I'll make sure you get them back as soon as I'm dressed,' said Joanna quickly. She noted the fingers already wearing several rings. 'You'll be wanting to add the ring to your collection.'

Lucille's eyes narrowed and she made no

128

move to leave. She had something else to say, and Joanna's heart sank still further.

'I think I ought to warn you, Miss Hamilton, about Matthew Howard. As you know, he is a very successful and talented film maker. He is surrounded by young and lovely girls wanting to be in his films. They would do anything, and I mean anything, to be cast for a part.' She paused to let this information sink in. 'If Matthew has said, or done anything, my dear, that you might misconstrue as interest on his part, then I must protect you, for your own sake.'

'How very kind,' said Joanna coolly. 'But I don't need your protection. If Matthew has just been amusing himself with my company, then surely you are aware that I have been doing the same. In my job, I meet men like him every day of the week. I have no illusions.'

It cost Joanna a great deal to dismiss her feelings for Matthew as if they were of no truth or depth; it was the only way to cope with Lucille's jealousy.

'Then that's all right,' said Lucille, rising. 'As long as you know that Matthew can mean nothing to you.' She hesitated. 'In fact, Matthew and I have a kind of understanding ... it goes back a long way, long before *Planet Eleven* actually, when he was working for my ex-husband. Matthew had a thing about me, even then. But he's so loyal, dear man ... however, when we get back to the States, he's promised me that everything will be in the open.'

'How nice,' said Joanna, opening the door.

'As long as you understand?' Lucille added in parting.

'Perfectly,' Joanna nodded.

In films, women threw themselves on double divans in paroxysms of weeping. Joanna did nothing like that. She stood, numbed, letting the misery seep right into her bones.

So the ring and the ivory box had been meant for Lucille; and the note ... what had it said:

'I will understand if you don't speak to me this morning. But don't send this back. It once belonged to a princess. Just give me a smile and I'll be happy.'

Something like that ... Joanna could not quite remember the words, but obviously Lucille had discovered the extent of Matthew's flirtation, perhaps they had even had words about it, and this was an 'I'm-sorry' present to make amends.

Joanna did not go downstairs for the buffet luncheon laid out by the pool. Any appetite had fled. She ordered some tea and nibbled at some fruit. She tried to do some work, but her mind kept returning to Matthew and Lucille. She had never really believed in the across-a-crowded-room syndrome, but she knew now

130

that it could happen. She was walking, weeping proof of it.

When had it happened? When had the sensible, hard-working woman journalist fallen for the man? When had it turned from attraction to love?

Joanna got up and went to the window. The Taj Mahal, pale and white, floated above the tree tops like something from outer space. It had been a very small moment when the knowledge came to her, when she realised that he was perfect for her, perfect in every way; someone who would give her freedom but be there to lean on; who would understand her mind and her feelings; who had strength, not weakness, who could be kind, a man blessed with both imagination and humour.

It was the moment when he gave her the little red bean.

She stood at the window, not seeing the Taj now for the blur of tears.

It was fitting for Joanna that she found the Red Fort at Agra a forbidding place. Their late afternoon visit suited her mood of gloom. It was within these seventy-foot high red sandstone walls that the Shah Jahan was held captive by his son Aurangzeb for seven years. The Moghuls could be very cruel. Legend has said that the Shah placed a mirror on his prison wall so that he could see his beloved Taj and the tomb of his wife. He died within the grim beauty of the palace fortress in 1666, his only solace being that now he would be with his Mumtaz Mahal.

Joanna remembered more of the journey back to the hotel. The Indian women were still working in the sandy rice fields on the banks of the river, their clothes tucked up. An old man smoked peacefully against the stump of a mango tree, his brown faced crumpled like a dried prune. Another woman stood in the muddy shallows, splashing water on the skinny naked body of her baby, perhaps to cool it more than for washing purposes. Further on a pair of bony buffalo were being scrubbed in the same water that they were drinking from, their leathery skins glistening and polished.

Joanna dressed with a great deal of care for dinner that night. There was one outfit in Mandy's prize wardrobe that she knew would look stunning on her. Nor did Mandy seem to mind lending it to her.

'Borrow anything you like,' said Mandy, flinging handfuls of bathsalts into the bath water. 'But will my things fit you? Pierre keeps saying how petite I am. I think tall men always like very small women, don't you? It makes them feel all hunky and protective.'

It was an outrageous harlequin taffeta evening suit made by one of the top London fashion designers. The trousers had nipped in ankles which Joanna wore pushed up to calf length as she was so much taller, with a neat jacket over a brief camisole top. She tied the belt round her hair and put on the gold mesh mules which had come with the amber dress. She looked like something from an eastern harem.

'Wow,' said Mandy, throwing clothes from her wardrobe all over the bed. 'I'm going to pass this evening. I can't compete with that. You look stunning.'

'Thanks,' said Joanna. 'At least I feel a little less like your aunt in this. I'm sorry if I boss you around, but you are my responsibility and you are, well, er—'

'A bit of a handful?' Mandy finished for her. 'I know. That's what my mother calls me. And she should know. She's brought me up single-handed since my dad died when I was eleven.'

'I'm sorry. I didn't know. I thought you had both parents.'

'That's all right. I hardly remember him now. I was upset at the time, my dad and all that. But now he's just someone in a photograph on the piano.'

'Your mother never thought of marrying again?'

'She hasn't had time. I've got a younger brother. She's been too busy working and looking after us. Besides, who'd take on a ready-made family these days. You'd have to be a saint.'

'Lots of people do.'

'Well, I've been talking to Matthew. I don't want to serve in a shop forever. I want to be in a movie, and he's a great director, isn't he? Perhaps he'll give me a chance. I know Andre thinks I'm really photo- photo—'

'Photogenic?'

'That's it. That's what he said. He said I was a natural.'

The natural went down to dinner in a frilly metallic silver ra-ra dress with bright shocking pink stockings and a feather boa. She certainly had her own ideas of how to wear the prize wardrobe. Together they made quite an entrance.

Matthew stood up and drew out two chairs. He was clearly amused by their appearances, but not unkindly.

'Amazing,' he said, lost for words for once. 'But why?'

'This is a celebration,' said Joanna.

'May we ask what you are celebrating?' said Andre.

'I'm celebrating a state of survival,' said Joanna, slipping into the chair furthest from Matthew. She could hide all her deepest hurt under a light, flippant tone. 'If I was in London, it would definitely be an evening for a champagne-crawl.'

Mandy giggled. 'I'm all for that. Sounds fantastic. Count me in on your next one, Joanna.'

'You're invited.'

Joanna worked all evening in a secluded corner of the comfortable lounge. She did not want to be completely isolated. From her armchair in the glow of a low lamp, she could watch the other tourists coming and going.

A steward arrived with a tray of iced drinks for her and she nodded her acknowledgment. She had no doubt that Matthew had placed the order. It was in his own interest that she had good working conditions, and a typical gesture.

She would never get any work done if his dark face dominated her mind. Mandy had been a pleasant companion today and it was easier to put herself in Mandy's shoes, writing the girl's diary for her impressions.

Later, exhausted, her mind dizzy with words, she closed her notebook and put it in her bag. She felt drained, by her work, and by the emotional turmoil of the day. It was an agony she had to conquer alone.

The gardens were marvellously cool and moonlit; the rickshaw boys had at last vanished and the road was empty. Joanna began to walk along it, downhill, through shady trees, their leaves rustling and silver in the moonlight. She felt quite safe walking along that country road, something she would not have done in England late at night.

She paused in the red stone entrance way, not really aware of anything, the darkness looming over her. Beyond the avenue of glass-like water was the Taj Mahal, thin as air, floating in the moonlight, its reflection

135

shimmering and ghostly in the still waters.

How did I get here, thought Joanna, dazed. She went down the steps to the watercourse, treading quietly, almost afraid to disturb the great stillness that hung over the gardens. Perhaps she would find the answer here where a love story had lived on for three hundred years.

Joanna now had the strangest feeling that the Taj could move. The more she thought about it, the more the idea took hold. A trick of light, the remaining heat haze, mist from the river . . . but it seemed that any moment the Taj might lift her marble lace skirts and float a few inches to the left or to the right. Perhaps she sometimes moved for those who believed in her, or perhaps by moonlight when she was quite alone.

She seemed to hear a voice, very far off, but sweet toned and sad. 'I'm glad you came,' said the voice. 'Glad you came . . .' The voice seemed to echo round the vaulted chamber and up into the soaring dome.

'I've been waiting such a long, long time,' said the imprisoned voice. 'I shall always be here, always be here . . .'

Poor little Mumtaz Mahal, thought Joanna. You are so very small to have this great weight above you.

How he must have loved you, this Shah Jahan, mighty Moghul emperor, man, lover, great architect. Was it worth dying, a beloved wife, to be enshrined in the most beautiful tomb in the world? Was it lonely before they brought him, at last understanding, to lie by your side?

Seven foot down they say you are, but you aren't. You are everywhere. In every corner of the gardens, in every inlaid jewel, in every crystal drop cascading from the fountains, even in the smallest crushed flower ... you are everywhere ...

Joanna did not know if she had been speaking her thoughts aloud. But her cheeks were wet with tears. She buried her head in her arms and wept. She knew that she loved Matthew desperately and hopelessly. She had waited all these years for a man to fill the emptiness in her heart, and now that she had found him, she would have to let him go. Matthew was not for her, and never could be. He lived in a different world.

A soft breeze stirred through her hair like comforting fingers. She lifted her face to the white vision.

She went down on her knees and dug a little hole in the earth with her nails. From her bag she took the little red bean, found the crack and opened it. She shook the hundred ivory elephants into the earth. They clung to the sides of the hole like motes of dust. She scooped back the earth, covering them, pressing them down with her knuckles, unable to understand why she was doing this, but knowing it was the only thing she could do.

It was symbolic. She was leaving her love for Matthew in these gardens. She had built for her love a Taj.

CHAPTER SEVEN

They were travelling west of Agra, twenty-four miles towards the rocky ridge on which Fatehpur Sikri was built in the 16th century. Matthew had hired an air conditioned de luxe coach to take the whole party, their drinks and equipment. He was not risking another nightmare drive like the one endured to Agra.

This was a morning trip to the ghost city, an imperial capital deep-frozen in time, abandoned by Emperor Akbar when the wells ran dry.

As they had the coach to themselves, there was plenty of room to spread out. Mandy flounced to the back of the coach and commandeered the whole of the back row. Lucille obviously planned to sit next to Matthew, but he put his briefcase on the seat beside him, opened it and began to work on some papers.

'What is the matter with our star this morning?' Andre asked as he took a seat across the aisle from Joanna.

She smiled and shook her head. Mandy was

in a very bad mood. 'You'll never believe it,' she said. 'Pierre laughed at her outfit. He didn't mean to upset her. He genuinely thought she looked funny.'

Andre dropped his voice to a whisper. 'Vraiment ... truly, she is wearing a most amusing outfit this morning. But where are all the beautiful clothes of her prize wardrobe?'

'She has decided that they are all crummy. That was her very word. So today she's wearing her own gear. Her words again.'

Andre nodded wisely. 'Gear is the only possible description.'

Mandy had come down to breakfast late. She had strolled into the dining room, her face set into an expression of indifference, her pretty mouth turned down.

Her own gear was a pair of combat trousers in ugly khaki greens and browns, many sizes too big, a man's ancient dinner jacket almost green with age over a tight boob tube in shiny black elastic lurex. To complete the total look against feminity, she had pushed all her hair inside a battered brown fedora which she wore pulled down on her forehead.

Pierre had, of course, laughed. It was a mistake.

As they sped over the dusty road Joanna marvelled again at the patience and toil of the Indian people, men and women, with their crude farming implements, the water wheel turned by a donkey or bullock, the old plough

139

pulled by a sluggish buffalo; the women washing by the village tank, the tethered goats; children playing using a stick for a bat, a clay bottle wrapped in rags for a doll, a paper kite or windmill.

Andre took photographs as they drove along. Children looked up and grinned and waved in a friendly way and ran alongside the coach till it outdistanced them. The women barely looked up from their work, except perhaps to draw a cloth to their face, or cover a wet limb. Women walked along the footpaths carrying pots on their heads, taking their husbands their mid-day meal of rice.

From where Joanna sat she could see Matthew's profile bent over his work, his dark hair curling damply into the nape of his tanned neck. She knew that hair was unbelievably thick and soft; her fingers had clawed through it in those moments of passion.

As they neared the deserted Moghul city, Joanna's courage returned. She had thought long and hard in the hours since she had buried her little red bean in the gardens of the Taj Mahal and wept so bitterly. She had to hide her love for Matthew. She had to put her very best efforts into her work; that in itself perhaps would help to ease the hurt.

Mandy got out of the coach with undisguised boredom. She trudged off in the opposite direction to the filming crew, sat down on a stone wall and began to read a crumpled magazine. She had not even spoken to Pierre, walking right past him with her nose in the air.

'Joanna,' Matthew called across to her. 'What are you going to do about Mandy? She's your responsibility. You'll have to speak to her. I'm not wasting the whole day because of her tantrums.'

'I'll go and see what's the matter,' said Joanna, speaking almost primly. 'Perhaps Mandy isn't well. It is hot, you know.'

'I appreciate that even Mandy is entitled to an off day. If that's the case, I'll be easy with the work, as long as she'll co-operate for a short time. Then she can go back to the coach, take an aspirin and lie down, or whatever.'

Again, Joanna was surprised by his understanding and kindness, despite the sternness in his voice and eyes.

But it was no longer any concern of hers . . . Matthew was just a man she had met, fleetingly, who had bowled her over with the magnetism of his personality. She needed time to breathe, to mentally get up and brush the dust off her sleeves.

'When will you be ready to start?' she heard herself asking.

'I'm planning to start right away. This light is perfect. I want to do a kind of somnolent sleeping beauty, fairy-tale sleep-walking track through the city. It's a sleeping city and I want to get that feeling of desolation and solitude.'

Andre was shouldering his camera ready to focus. Pierre's sound receiver hung from his shoulder. His young face had a look of bewilderment. He could not understand Mandy's extreme reaction. He had only laughed, a little laugh, only half a laugh really. The microphone was slipping in his uncertain hands; he wiped them down the side of his jeans. He could not afford to have a wiring fault.

Lucille had brought a parasol with her to keep off the sun. Her appearance was band-box as usual, not a hair out of place. It was not possible to see her eyes behind her large modish sun-glasses as she chalked the next take number on the clapperboard.

'Do you feel like starting now?' said Joanna casually, very low key. 'Matthew says he'll make this an easy morning. Even budding TV stars get a half day apparently,' she added lightly.

'I'm not going round any more boring ruins,' said Mandy, not looking up from the page she was reading. 'I'm sick of ruins.'

'All he wants you to do is to walk through the city as if in a dream,' Joanna went on as if she had not heard Mandy. 'Like sleep-walking. It's a fascinating place, quite untouched by time; you might even enjoy it ... the Mint, the Astrologer's Seat, the Human Chessboard...'

'The what?'

'When the Emperor Akbar was bored he

played chess with slave girls as living pieces on a huge chessboard in a courtyard.'

'Really weird,' said Mandy, yawning. 'Nut case.'

'Every day the astrologer would tell the Emperor what colour to wear. And there's another building full of stone monsters where the Emperor used to play hide and seek with the ladies of his harem,' said Joanna, trying to generate interest.

'Weirder and weirder,' said Mandy. 'What was this guy? Some freaky drop-out?'

'I doubt if that is exactly how the historians would care to describe this Moghul Emperor. So, just a little stroll through the city, and then you can do what you like. Coming?'

'Do I have to?'

'Well, if you want to impress Matthew with your dedication to his film making, then I should co-operate if I were you. Didn't you say something about hoping he might cast you in something in the future? He's being very understanding.'

'Okay,' said Mandy, rising. She pulled off the brown fedora and shook out her hair. Joanna had to swallow her gasp of horror. The girl had dyed her pretty fair curls to a bright magenta shade. She looked like a parrot. A sulky parrot at that.

'Okay,' said Mandy again, walking over to Matthew, her eyes defying anyone to comment. 'What do you want me to do? Let's get cracking. I'm sick of this place already.'

There was a stunned silence and then everyone began talking at once. Even Pierre cheered up. He suddenly saw Mandy as she really was, a child acting grown-up. Joanna saw some of the tenseness go from his hunched shoulders and was relieved.

'Are you furious?' she murmured to Matthew when she had a chance. She felt guilty about the brilliant crimson hair, though she could not be expected to keep tabs on everything Mandy did in her room.

'I'm wild about it,' said Matthew flippantly.

'I'm really sorry.'

'Don't be so meek. It's not your fault. Hey, Lucille, give Mandy your parasol,' he ordered in the same voice he had used to Joanna many times. He squinted down the lens. 'Yes, that's it. Baggy combat trousers, magenta punk hair and a frilly Parisian parasol ... perfect. Our Mandy has done the trick again. I couldn't have asked for a better contrast to this sleeping city. Let me line up.'

The human chessboard was in the courtyard of Diwan-i-Am, the Hall of Public Audiences, and here Joanna found herself suddenly pulled onto one of the fading and bleached flagstones of the board. Less reluctantly Lucille was also asked to stand as a chess piece where the Emperor had once used his slavegirls. Matthew called out the moves and the three women obeyed his commands in the growing

144

heat, limply and lethargically. 'Camera,' he drawled.

'I don't know what I'm supposed to do,' Mandy grumbled.

'Move sideways,' Joanna whispered. 'One square.'

She felt almost sated with history. There was so much to see. The tomb of the saint Shaikh Salim Chisti under an elaborate mother-of-pearl canopy where thousands of childless Hindu and Moslem women came to pray for the blessing of a child. The strange stone column in the Hall of Private Audience, topped with a carved stone flower, which was the Emperor's throne, connected to surrounding galleries by four stone bridges. He sat far above the people of his court, with them, but not mingling.

A morning was just not enough time, but everyone was tiring, especially Mandy. There were refrigerated cold drinks in the coach, and Matthew let her go back for her favourite coke.

'I've just a few long shots to take. Joanna, put on Mandy's baggy trousers and take the parasol. At a distance, no one will notice the difference.'

Joanna felt her colour rising. 'Me? In those trousers? Never.' She was outraged.

'Don't be so ridiculously pompous,' he said exasperated. 'I haven't asked you to strip off. No one will know it's you,' he added heaping on the insults. 'Mandy's done very well this

145

morning, and I'm not risking tomorrow's work by overdoing it here.'

Joanna climbed into the coach, fighting to control her anger. Mandy looked up, guardedly.

'I've got to wear your trousers,' Joanna blurted out. 'I'm your stand-in apparently. That man is a monster. He thinks he can just order people around as if they were ... they were...'

'Slave girls?' Mandy suggested, slipping out of the combat trousers. Joanna unzipped her own sleek white linen culottes, and stepped into the baggy pants. She felt like Charlie Chaplin. It was humiliating. a fleeting expression of sympathy crossed Mandy's face.

'You don't look that bad,' she said cheerfully. 'Could be worse. He could have ordered you to dye your hair.'

Joanna stomped out of the coach. All her dignity and cool had gone. She snatched up the parasol and began walking away from the camera. She bet Lucille was just loving this.

'How far do you want me to go?' she yelled. 'Sir.'

'Over there. On the ridge. Get it?'

It was a long walk. It was hot and several times she stumbled over loose stones and the descending folds of the trousers. In her anger she had snapped the elastic round the waist. It had every indication of turning into a farce as she struggled to keep the flapping trousers decently in place, and hold the parasol up. She needed another pair of hands.

The Emperor's games had nothing on the one Matthew was playing now. He ordered her here and there. She trudged along in the heat, perspiration streaming off her body. Her eyes were gritty from dust. Again she stumbled as her heel caught in a hole. She flung out her arm to save herself falling, and the parasol lifted in the breeze and turned a somersault down the incline.

Instinctively she tried to catch it, forgetting the trousers, which fell down round her ankles in voluminous folds. She staggered hopelessly, crumbling onto the rough stones into a furiously weeping heap of womanhood.

She heard someone running over the uneven ground. She was hurt and angry, as much angry with herself as with Matthew who had inflicted this on her.

'Go away. Go away,' she cried fiercely.

'Are you hurt?' asked Matthew's voice, from some distance.

'What do you care?' she snapped, her eyes flashing. 'I could have broken every bone, all for a stupid long shot. Will you go away? I can manage quite well by myself.'

He was scrambling up the slope. 'I doubt it,' he panted. He had been running, and surveyed her dishevelment with a wicked gleam.

'Well, well, this really is one for the home movies,' he grinned.

'If you're filming this, I'll sue you,' she exploded. 'Isn't it enough that you've made a laughing stock of me? Now go away, you've had your fun. Allow me to return to the coach, and my own clothes, with some dignity.'

He slid an arm round her waist and helped her to her feet, then bent to retrieve the baggy trousers. Joanna fought to reclothe herself, but he was calmly folding the excess material round her middle, and making a big tuck like a sari.

'Don't struggle,' he said. 'Do you want everyone to see your lacy bikini pants? Very fetching they are too, Joanna. You have delightful taste, underneath.'

Joanna's eyes held a look of incredulity. He could humiliate her in this way, and still pile on the baiting. It was inhuman. She could have struck him, but two things stopped her. Firstly the knowledge that it would do no good except to give vent to her feelings; secondly, she had hurt her wrist.

A shooting pain was going up her right forearm. She remembered putting out her hand to break her fall, and coming down on it awkwardly. She winced as she tentatively moved her fingers. At least she had not broken her wrist.

He turned her chin and forced her to look straight at him. His eyes hardened briefly. 'You have hurt yourself,' he said. 'Nothing escapes me. You should know that by now.'

'It's just my wrist. I've sprained it a bit. I tried to stop myself falling...'

He took her hand very gently and turned it over. He ran his thumb over the swelling, then rotated the wrist to its normal movement. 'I've got horses,' he said. 'I know about sprains.'

'Oh, Matthew,' she said, half crying, half laughing. 'You really are the limit. Now you are comparing me to a horse!'

The mixture of emotions that she had gone through in the last few minutes were suddenly too much for Joanna to sort out. She started laughing, lightly at first, then helplessly, leaning against Matthew as if he were just a lamp post in the street.

Matthew began to laugh too, that dark deep sound that she loved, and before either of them knew what was happening, their arms were around her each other and their mouths opening into a kiss that drained the resistance from their bodies. It was a kiss that blocked all thought. It was a kiss that tore down every barrier that had existed. It had an intensity that neither of them had ever experienced before.

They leaned against each other, shaken, trembling, the sun beating down on them in the deserted city.

'Today I went sleep-walking in a city that won't ever wake up,' said Joanna softly.

'What?' His mouth was against her hair.

'Mandy's Diary,' she said. 'The first line of Mandy's Diary for today.'

'Damn Mandy's Diary,' he said, huskily, turning her face towards him again and kissing her. 'You're the only person I care about. Are you going to stop leading me such a hell of a dance now? You've been driving me crazy. Hot one minute, cold the next ... please, Joanna, if you're the kind of sweet, loving person, I think you are, no more games.'

'But Matthew,' Joanna protested. 'I thought it was you who were playing games. You know, a holiday conquest, one more notch on your belt, an English novelty. I couldn't stand it. That's why I tried to put you right out of my mind.'

'And you couldn't succeed?' he teased.

She shook her head, the sunlight catching the red streaks in her chestnut hair. 'It was impossible. I love you too much.'

He held her closely against his chest, a warm, protective safe embrace that made Joanna feel that the outside world had ceased to exist.

'And I love you, Joanna darling. You've no idea how long I've been waiting for you. Like the Shah Jahan I've been looking into a mirror, the mirror of life, every day, hoping that soon I would meet you. I wanted someone real and human, not a cardboard Hollywood starlet. I wanted a real woman with fire and spirit, with courage and determination.'

'And is that me?' asked Joanna, her eyes dancing. 'All those things?'

'And many many more,' said Matthew. 'It's

150

going to take me a lifetime to tell you about them.'

He twined her arms around him and they kissed again. They knew nothing would ever be the same again. They were in a state of euphoria, their hands touching, their eyes meeting constantly, full of love towards each other.

He helped her down the slope and they walked slowly back towards the coach, no eyes now for the magnificent palaces and mosques of the Emperor Akbar. They were laughing, and Matthew held her good hand. Her other wrist was hurting but it was right at the back of her mind.

As they neared the film crew they realised that they had been less than discreet. A few Indian pilgrims turned away with shy smiles. Pierre was grinning. Andre was shaking his head in mock disapproval. Mandy was jogging about in the back of the coach, giving Joanna a thumbs up sign and miming applause.

Only Lucille was not amused. Her face was drawn and bitter. She looked at Joanna with hatred and malice. Joanna saw the older woman's expression and a tremor of fear touched her happiness.

'Okay folks, the floor show's over,' said Matthew, quite undisturbed by their audience. His arm was round Joanna's shoulder now; no one was taking any notice of her silly outfit. 'Let's wrap it up here, and get back to the hotel.

Joanna has hurt her wrist and I want to get a doctor to look at it.'

Mandy came discoing down to the front of the coach.

'That was fantastic,' she gabbled. 'Just like a scene from *Gone With the Wind* or *Casablanca*. It was so romantic!' She lowered her voice about one decibel and spoke to Joanna. 'I'm glad you beat that old she-tiger. She's been trying to eat him alive for days.'

It did not help that Lucille heard Mandy's remarks. She-tiger was right, Joanna thought; she had never seen a woman looking so dangerous.

Matthew gave the driver instructions to return to the Clark's Shiraz. He abandoned his seat at the front and his briefcase, and came to sit beside Joanna, immediately taking her hand into his. It was like being a teenager all over again. She remembered the times Bruce had held her hand and for once the memory was not overwhelmed by awful sadness. She thought briefly of their happy times, before the accident, and that was good.

'Now,' said Matthew as they drove along the road back to Agra, 'I hope there will be no more nonsense and you'll wear the ruby ring I gave you yesterday.'

'The ring?' Her voice seemed to give a little wild leap. 'You mean the ruby ring in the ivory box?' she repeated idiotically.

He shot her a look of amused patience. 'Are

you sure you didn't bump your head? A mild case of concussion perhaps?'

'I'm just a little surprised,' said Joanna, unsteadily. 'You see, although I thought at first they were gifts for me—well, later I discovered from Lucille they were meant to be delivered to her.'

'Lucille was there when I gave the package to the head waiter and asked him to give it to you when you came down to breakfast. Perhaps she was curious and went into the shop to find out what I had bought.'

'But there was the note inside.'

'She knows I never sign anything, nor put a name. She would know this from the countless reminders I send her. So she took a chance. It all seems pointless to me,' he added. 'Where's the ring now?'

'I gave it to her.'

He began to laugh. 'That's really neat. You are the dearest, gullible little innocent. You must start to mistrust people. I don't understand why. Lucille must have dozens of rings; her husband gave her jewels of every kind.'

Joanna thought deeply, wondering how much to tell him. She did not want to spoil their wonderful new closeness by relating Lucille's warning.

'I don't think it was so much the ring,' said Joanna carefully, 'but primarily the idea of a gift. She wanted it to be seen that you gave her gifts, to prove her worth, your friendship. She did not want me to receive a gift, or I might start to think I was someone special—'

'You are,' he interrupted.

'In a way, she was putting me in my place.'

'Rather clumsily,' said Matthew. 'Darling, shall I get it back from her, or shall we let her keep the ruby?'

'Let her keep it,' said Joanna, smiling up at him.

His dark eyes warmed appreciatively. 'I knew you'd say that. You have a generous heart. I have decided anyway, having seen how slim your fingers are...' he lifted them to his lips for a kiss... 'that the antique ring was too heavy for you. I shall buy you a diamond, light and sparkling and full of the colours of the air.'

'I'd like that,' said Joanna softly. 'But Matthew, aren't we going ahead a little too fast? No one has said anything about rings or commitments. A few kisses do not a commitment make.'

'Do you want me to go down on one knee?' he demanded. 'Do you want all the frills, the declaration of love, a formal proposal? I thought you were a modern young woman.'

'Please ... I'm confused,' said Joanna. She did not know where for the time being this love was taking her, or where they stood. 'Can we leave it for the moment? I've a lot to think about.'

'As long as you like,' he said. 'But remember,

I've been waiting years. And now that I've found you, I've become a very impatient man. I don't want to waste a minute.'

Along the road were strange conical piles about twenty feet high. They were kos minars, milestones put there by the Moghuls. They towered above the coach sentry-like, impassive, marking time as well as distance. She would never forget India. It was turning into a magic carpet for her as well. She did not know if she had any future within Matthew. For the moment it was enough to know that he loved her.

At the hotel, Matthew strode ahead, wanting to put in a call for a doctor. If they could not provide one, he was quite adamant about flying Joanna back to Delhi for treatment.

As they were leaving the coach, there was a silly incident. Lucille stabbed Joanna's foot with the point of her parasol. She pretended it was an accident.

'My dear, I'm sorry, terribly sorry!' Lucille fluttered and showed concern, but Joanna was not taken in. She wanted to say something really cutting: 'Oh by the way, Lucille, Matthew is so glad you like the ring. He says you're to keep it.'

She would have enjoyed saying that, but something warned her to keep quiet. It might be more to her advantage to keep Lucille wondering whether Matthew knew of the transfer of the gift. Joanna sighed ... she wanted life to be simple and straightforward. It took so much more energy to be devious.

The doctor was swift to arrive at the hotel; tourist injuries were the only lucrative part of his practice. He examined Joanna's wrist and said it was a simple sprain. He prescribed a few days rest, an elastic bandage for support and some pain-killers.

A spot of blood was welling on her foot where the ferrule had jabbed the flesh; Joanna drew it slowly out of sight, and tucked it behind the other one. She did not want Matthew making any inquiries.

'I'm feeling much better already,' said Joanna.

'I think you're being very brave,' said Mandy stoutly, who had suddenly become very pro-Joanna. She was excited by the thought of romance and by Lucille's obvious hostility. She knew Joanna had a kind heart, and she might well put in a word for her with Matthew. The way to fame was still open. She felt quite elated. 'You're not to do any more work.'

'Of course, I've got to work,' said Joanna. 'I'm not exactly at death's door. Although I could always get a typewriter from the hotel, and you could type up my notes for me,' she added mischievously. 'That would be a great help.'

'My typing's rotten,' said Mandy,

disappearing with a wooden smile towards the pool.

Matthew and Joanna both laughed. He took her good hand. 'So much for Mandy's sympathy,' he grinned. 'I'll give you ten minutes to change then we're going to lunch together. I've booked a table for two. No intruders for our first lunch together. Just you and me, and the future to talk about.'

Joanna sighed happily. 'How lovely. Just you and me and lunch, but no future, Matthew. Let's just keep it to the present.'

'As you wish,' he said, bending to kiss her fingers, but his eyes were fathomless and shadowed.

She changed into her prettiest dress, pale buttercup silk with a pleated skirt and floppy silk bow from the collar. She put on the gold mesh mules again, which seemed right even with this afternoon outfit.

There was a yellow orchid by her plate. She did not pin it to her dress, but stood it in a glass of water. Its petals were very thin and fragile, streaked with coral, pale and waxy.

'Thank you,' she said, as she sat down on the chair he held out for her. 'I love flowers.'

'It's going to be flowers all the way,' he said. 'Even if you do just stick them in a glass of water.'

The lunch was delicious ... a cold soup, tandoori chicken, and a fruit salad of gauvas and mango, sliced in a sweet spiced sauce.

'And I'm laying on champagne from here to LA,' he promised. 'I'm going to enjoy spoiling you, my darling. I want to give you everything you want.'

'And that isn't one big shopping spree,' said Joanna firmly.

'What a pity,' he said lazily. 'I thought you were marrying me for my money.'

She tried to keep her face quite expressionless, and her voice light. He was ordering her about again, planning her life.

'Dearest Matthew,' she said. 'I'm not going to LA. I've got a job in London which I have to go back to. And please, I don't want to talk about marriage.'

'You needn't talk about it,' he agreed. 'But it won't stop me talking about marriage, our marriage. You'd better get used to the idea, because it's going to happen.'

'I know,' she said softly. 'It's going to happen.'

He leaned across the table, taking her hand and began to run his fingertip up and down over the sensitive skin of her fingers. It was so light a touch, it sent shivers down her spine.

'And what does a prim young English journalist think about love in the afternoon?' he asked evenly, though his dark eyes were dancing.

'I've never really thought about it,' said Joanna, taken by surprise. 'For a start, it would have to be somewhere very, very special, and with someone quite extraordinary,' said Joanna, keeping her voice light. 'I should imagine that daylight could be quite inhibiting...'

'Tell me about that very, very special somewhere,' he said, still tracing her fingers.

'It has to be a really beautiful room with lovely comfortable furniture. It has to be warm and full of sunshine and yet cool at the same time. If there could be flowers and the sound of birds singing...'

'Anything else?'

'Oh, yes. The room has to have a view of the Taj Mahal.'

'A tall order,' he said.

'Almost impossible,' Joanna agreed.

'But, of course, if the someone was quite an extraordinary person—'

'Then he might even manage the Taj Mahal,' Joanna finished for him.

They left the empty dining room hands entwined, walking upstairs and not taking the lift because these magical moments of anticipation were ones to be lingered over. Joanna was acutely aware of his height, his warmth, the texture of his skin. Matthew was like a rock beside her ... steady, strong, steadfast.

He took her to his room and across to the window where the Taj stood mistily and white behind the tree tops. The gardens were bathed in sunlight and the birds fluttered within the cool branches of the flowering trees. He drew her into his arms and touched her lips gently. She stood quite still as he sought the fastenings of her dress and it slipped from her bare shoulders.

'I promise you splendour,' he said softly. 'My darling Joanna.'

The wild winds of desire stirred, then swept through them as their lips met in a kiss that crushed all ability to breathe. Joanna sobbed for air, and yet clung to him, eager for more of his kisses, her senses reeling, her elation growing, drawing his head down to her own moist mouth.

He carried her to the bed, caressing her skin with a tenderness and passion that had her moaning with delight. Matthew was everything that a lover should be. Her joy was almost complete …

'I love you, I love you,' Joanna whispered against his hair as waves of sensation took over her body. Suddenly it was as if she exploded into tiny atoms and she was sent flying into the bursting sun. The roaring fire scorched her skin. Her heels had wings. They soared together into the heights, a rainbow dazzle of lights beneath their eyes.

Matthew had kept his promise.

CHAPTER EIGHT

After a morning of re-shooting some of the film, Matthew took Joanna to the tiny, fairy-tale palace of Itimad-ud-Daulah which the Lady of the Taj had built in memory of her grandparents. They needed to be away from the others; to be together for a few hours.

'Is it very far?' Joanna asked. Mandy had been unusually quiet all morning. 'You know I don't like leaving Mandy for too long.'

'It's the other side of town. We'll take a rickshaw. I want to talk to you, darling. We deserve some time on our own,' he insisted.

Outside the doves were cooing in the shade of trees in the hotel garden. Birds circled endlessly in the sky, kites, mynahs and sparrows. Joanna smiled at Matthew, still amazed that he loved her, that he wanted her.

They hired the handsome youth with the clean shirt and decorated canopy. The ragged boy also waited, leaning dejectedly against his battered bicycle, chewing and spitting. He had not had a fare all day. But he was not strong enough to pull two grown people, even though he would try.

'Hang on,' Matthew laughed as they tilted forward. 'I've got you. You won't fall off.'

Joanna gasped as the boy set off at a great pace and the rickshaw rocked from side to side.

She held onto Matthew's shirt, laughing, and they clung together, quite unaware that they were being watched from a hotel window.

She had never been so happy. Their love-making had been perfect, and afterwards Matthew had looked her straight in the eye, and there was no regret or guilt or embarrassment, only warmth and tenderness. Now they were alone again. She felt that they were escaping from the demands of Fleet Street, television and Hollywood as the rickshaw clattered down the long avenue into the busy town.

The colourful sights, sounds and smells of Agra crowded before them. It was a busy, bustling, industrial town thronged with people and beasts plodding the narrow streets. It had quite a distinct life from the Taj; a shamble of monuments, shacks and tumbledown houses, stores and markets, every wall pasted with political posters, torn and faded, shreds fluttering in the breeze. A dusty train rumbled in from Delhi, crowded beyond belief, passengers almost spilling from the windows.

She leaned precariously from the rickshaw, one arm curved round the canopy pole, the other safely anchored within Matthew's grasp. She turned and smiled at him. He understood. There was so much to see, and so little time. She caught sight of a car and a private car was a rare thing in Agra, decked with garlands of marigolds for a wedding.

They passed children on a street corner eating cones of shaved ice topped with vivid green syrup; a camel plodded along in the gutter, laden with sacks. The wheelwrights squatted at their hammering, the baker shovelled hot ashes into the street, straight from his ovens; a fishmonger gutted fish on the pavement, slitting them open on a huge blade wedged in a stone.

Strange smells floated across from the sweetmeat shop, sticky and sickly; baskets heaped with flowers lined the roadside; cyclists and buffalo cut in on them from side lanes, the great beasts sweating and blowing at the flies.

The rickshaw boy knew many people. He called out greetings, waving, grinning at the replies.

'They are all saying how lucky I am to have such a beautiful woman by my side,' said Matthew, faintly teasing. Joanna's smile deepened.

'And no doubt estimating the number of children we'll produce,' she said. 'A large family is considered a security for the future.'

'I want lots of children to look after me when I'm old,' said Matthew. 'For security reasons.'

'No doubt,' said Joanna, demurely, refusing to be drawn.

The sun beat down. They passed another rickshaw where the boy was pulling four passengers, his knees almost buckling under the strain. Joanna's heart contracted with pity, and she felt Matthew's grip tighten.

'There's nothing you can do,' he said, close to her. 'You can't change India. He may be quite happy in his own way. Give him one of your sweet smiles, Joanna. It'll make his day. The same as it makes mine...'

She curled her fingers in his so that he would know that he was helping just by being there. So much time had been wasted; years had gone by. She wanted to feel every emotion deeply, to feel alive again. Even her toes were tingling. She leaned against him, not caring what Matthew thought of her. This afternoon was theirs; she wanted to remember every sensation.

Itimad-ud-Daulah lay on the other side of the river, three miles north of the Taj. They crossed the long bridge over the Holy Jamna. The bed had dried up to a narrow central flow, shallow and dirty, waiting for the rains. The fertile earth on the river bed was sprouting green where the Indian farmers were making use of its richness. Buffalo cooled their heels in a few inches of water. Dhobis squatted at the water's edge, bashing the clothes against a rock, scrubbing with a tablet of coarse yellow soap. Turtles swam lazily, diving into murky mud. Some near naked boys were laughing and splashing each other.

It was a garden tomb, by the river, so small by comparison to the Taj that it seemed like a dolls house. It was a perfect gem, wonderfully proportioned, the personality of the little Queen who had it built evident in its glowing white marble lacework.

They went through a gate near the river, hand in hand. It was inlaid with semi-precious stones in mosaics over almost its entire surface. But it was not a sad place like the Taj; it was happy with spring-like pictures of trees, flowers and fruit, wine cups and flagons. It was so easy to imagine Mumtaz Mahal walking through these same gardens, planning and designing, the same sun shining on her labour of love, not knowing that she was building the forerunner of her own tomb.

'I'm sure that the Shah Jahan came here when his wife died, in those first days,' said Joanna. 'He looked across this same river and wondered how to fill the empty years. Then he looked at this perfect little tomb, and was inspired to build the Taj Mahal.'

'Joanna, I'm going to have to take you home soon,' said Matthew sternly. 'You are beginning to get India in your bloodstream. You need a short, sharp dose of London or Paris. Yes, I'm sure that's the cure ... a week-end in Paris at one of the world's most elegant hotels. Shall we go there the moment this filming is finished?'

'I have to get back to the *Daily Post*.'

'Doesn't your editor give you any time off?' he said impatiently. 'You're not a slave.'

'My job's important to me,' she answered.

'Would you give up your career if I asked you to?'

'But that's different,' he said, the muscles of his face tightening.

'It's only different in that you're famous and successful in your field, whereas I'm comparatively low on the ladder. But still, Fleet Street is an achievement and I worked hard to get there.'

'You need never work again,' Matthew insisted, making her look into his eyes. They were so dark and intense that Joanna felt her resolve slipping. It would be only too simple just to give in to Matthew. 'Don't you understand that, you independent young woman?'

The garden was very peaceful. Joanna and Matthew were the only visitors to the forgotten tomb. The unexplorable blue stretched beyond their vision.

A cooling breeze from the river touched her bare arms and she shivered. 'Let's go back, Matthew. It gets dark so quickly and I don't fancy being stranded in Agra town at night.'

The youth was waiting for them. He deftly wheeled his bicycle round and mounted for the long ride back. They got caught in the homeward traffic of carts, cyclists and shambling lorries, rattling and falling to pieces.

They were surrounded by beggars as they waited, dirty, whining children with sores and running eyes. Matthew threw some coins onto the footpath, hoping this would make them disperse, but it was a mistake. More appeared like magic, their shrill voices cutting the evening air, thin brown arms stretched out. The rickshaw boy shouted at them, guarding his precious vehicle from their inquisitive fingers.

'This is one aspect of India that I could never get used to,' said Joanna, ashamed of her own feelings.

'It's life,' said Matthew.

At last they were on the move. The youth took them back a different way, skirting the massively towering walls of the Red Fort where the Shah Jahan had been imprisoned. Joanna was immediately reminded of the mirror on his cell wall, reflecting the Taj, and was again saddened by human cruelty.

'You can't right all wrongs, my darling,' said Matthew, sensing her thoughts. 'I suppose as soon as you get your hands on my money, you'll give it all away. Ah, well...'

'Oh Matthew, please don't keep talking as if it's all settled. I don't want to decide anything. I'm so happy now, I just want to stay that way.'

'Of course, I could sell my second Rolls and let you give that away. After all, two is a trifle extravagant.'

'Matthew, you're quite hopeless. I can't equate your wealth with this poverty. It's beyond me to know what to do.'

'Tomorrow I'm taking you to the Lake

Palace at Upaipur. Joanna, it's so beautiful . . . a dream of white marble rising from the blue water of the lake. And although the palace is now a hotel, it's still furnished with heirlooms and valuable works of art.'

'You're not taking me,' Joanna corrected gently. 'The *Daily Post* is.'

'A figure of speech.' He did not like admitting that he was not totally responsible for their plans. He wanted to map her life, take care of her, pay for everything. Joanna sensed this. It seemed to her that Matthew equated love with possession.

As they turned into the drive of the hotel, they saw Lucille standing in the entrance way, leaning elegantly but stiffly on her parasol. Andre was also there. They seemed to be arguing.

'At last,' Lucille fumed, hurrying over. 'Trust you two to disappear just when you're wanted. I've been trying to locate you for over an hour. No one knew where you'd gone.'

'Why? What's the matter?' Joanna asked, but already a small chill of apprehension touched her. There was no mistaking the look of triumph on Lucille's face; by contrast Andre looked worried.

'It's your precious Magic Carpet girl,' said Lucille, swinging round. 'She's hopped on her magic carpet again and flown. Only this time she's taken our sound man with her. Matthew will be quite unable to finish his film.'

'They've gone,' Andre echoed. 'They must have packed their things and caught the afternoon express back to Delhi.'

'Are you sure?' Matthew snapped. 'Perhaps they've just gone out for a drive.'

'With all their luggage? No, they've cleared off and left you high and dry,' said Lucille, her eyes glinting.

'I don't believe it,' said Joanna, trying to control the dismay in her voice. 'Pierre is a responsible person even if Mandy is a bit wild.'

'She's a scheming little minx,' said Lucille. There was a flush of excitement on the mask of her make-up. She was glad that Matthew's work was halted, incomplete. She wanted the whole Indian episode over so that she and Matthew could return to the States.

'If they have, it's unforgivable,' said Matthew, striding into the hotel, fuming. 'Udaipur is a vital part of the film; the contrast of the lake city to all this sandstone and vast plains.'

'It's Joanna's fault,' Lucille went on, following Matthew like a prim manicured poodle on a lead. 'She encouraged this youthful romance. She practically threw Mandy at Pierre's head.'

'That's not true,' said Joanna hotly. 'Pierre was just as interested in Mandy. And I was glad because it made her happier. She was very homesick and the first lot of filming was a nightmare. But once she and Pierre got together, Mandy began to co-operate.'

'Got together?' Lucille sneered. 'Is that how you put it? In America we have a different expression.'

'Joanna's right,' said Andre. 'Pierre made the running. He's not exactly a monk and Mandy's a pretty girl. I'm far more concerned about what they might be rushing into. A few days in India together is no basis for a marriage.'

He might have been speaking about Joanna and Matthew. The same wisdom applied to them, but at that moment neither of them could dwell on it. Matthew was inquiring at the reception desk for messages. He came back with an envelope, his face grim.

'It's for you,' he said, thrusting it at Joanna.

Joanna recognised Mandy's large immature handwriting on the envelope, and tore it open.

'Pierre and I have eloped,' she read out. 'Isn't it romantic? And very French. Don't worry about me. Love Mandy.'

'I told you so,' said Lucille inclining her head.

'This is quite disastrous.' Matthew was pacing the foyer floor. 'That girl was your responsibility, Joanna. Why couldn't you have kept a firmer control of her? That was your job.'

'Oh, you—' Joanna was shattered by his sudden attack. 'How unfair.'

'I'm sure Joanna didn't need any persuading

170

to leave Mandy alone,' said Lucille smoothly. 'I've seen her going out quite a few times. There's no need to have it on your conscience, Matthew darling.'

'They ordered a taxi. They didn't cover their tracks. It was all very open.' Andre was almost talking to himself. He looked weary.

'Open?' Lucille scoffed. 'You mean being devious. No doubt the taxi was re-routed to the airport once they left the hotel.'

'I can soon find out,' said Matthew. 'I suggest we return to Delhi immediately. I'll check whether they are booked onto a flight to London or the States.'

'Some major airlines touch down at Bombay,' Joanna suggested. 'They might think it romantic to go to Bombay.'

She stressed the word romantic, but Matthew was looking at her as if she were a stranger, an annoying stranger. The tender lover had vanished. He had reverted to the tough film maker who allowed nothing to go wrong.

'I'll check that too. Joanna, will you go and throw my things into a case,' he ordered. 'I take it you can cope? Perhaps you are more efficient at packing than taking care of your charge.'

Joanna did not answer. He tossed his key to her.

'Why, I'll pack for you,' said Lucille laying on the charm. 'Mine won't take a moment. I brought so little with me.' For someone who

171

had worn a different outfit for every period of the day, this was something of an understatement.

'You're not coming,' said Matthew, wiping the smile from her face with four words. 'You and Andre are going to Udaipur. You've been wanting to try your hand at filming. This is your chance. I want you to film everything in sight. If I can use five per cent of it, I'll be lucky. Now, bring your notebook and I'll tell you what shots to look out for.'

He propelled Lucille into a deserted corner of the lounge, leaving Joanna fuming with the key to his room. She packed his clothes like a robot, swiftly and remotely, trying not to remember the intimacy of those moments shared in this room. She avoided looking at the bed.

But her heart turned over as his possessions revealed yet another side of his complex character; a battered alarm clock that must have accompanied him for years as he trekked the world filming; a paperback copy of Darwin's Life, well thumbed; an electric toothbrush; no pyjamas.

She was folding his white tuxedo jacket when her fingers felt a hard object in a pocket. She knew what it was without taking it out. It was the amber elephant he had taken from the table at the Amber Palace. She wondered why he had never given it to her. Presumably he had bought it for her, and yet it remained forgotten in his pocket.

Joanna blinked back her tears. As quickly forgotten as she was going to be. Matthew had not meant what he had said to her. His films always came first. She had just been a pleasant diversion in a hot climate ... it was cruel.

Her own packing took even less time. She had never expected to leave Agra like this, almost in disgrace. She swept everything into her cases with little regard for creases, then made a quick tour of Mandy's room. She picked up a sandal from under the bed, a wet bikini and a whole range of jars and bottles from the bathroom.

She rang for a boy to come up for the cases, then left the suite. Again, she only had memories for the future. Bruce and she had taken it for granted that they had a future and the carefree days of their youth were blurred and hazy. She had not collected memories then. But she remembered that last evening so clearly she could almost smell the fog mixed with the scent of wet leaves that left the roads greasy and treacherous. They did not have to tell her. She knew that he was dead.

Matthew was using the telephone in the foyer, his hand cupped over the earpiece. It was obviously a bad line. His eyes were like granite.

'I hope I've done your packing to your satisfaction,' said Joanna, tossing him the key.

'Be quiet. I can't hear.'

He deliberately turned, silencing her with

173

the movement, and Joanna was left looking at his broad back. She might be going to Delhi with him, but it was not going to be a pleasure trip. She wandered over to the hotel shops. A good book might be an idea for the journey.

It came as no surprise to find Lucille waiting for her. Her face was composed now, her lips outlined in dark plum lipstick and Joanna was immediately reminded of the wicked queen in *Snow White*.

'Joanna,' she said. 'I think it's time we had another talk. Perhaps I didn't make myself quite clear yesterday.'

Joanna stifled a sigh. She did not want to talk to Lucille. She did not want to talk to anyone. She felt hurt and raw.

'I don't have time,' said Joanna. 'We're leaving right away.'

'I think you'd better make time. Come outside. I don't want us to be overheard.'

Joanna followed the older woman, almost mesmerised. What could she possibly have to say that mattered now? Matthew had made it clear that his work was the most important part of his life.

The Indian dusk was claiming the light and the full scent of the flowers was heavy in the air. Birds were roosting. The peacock's cry was like a cat as it stalked the grass, its tail fanned out in turquoise and purple blue magnificence.

She had almost forgotten the Taj during this day with Matthew, but Mumtaz Mahal would forgive her. She, of all people, would understand about love, and the special awareness of the first beginnings.

But the dome of the Taj was there now, sad and ghostly, ready for another good-bye. Joanna was hardly listening to Lucille, her thoughts and feelings far more concerned with the beauty that she was leaving.

'And so you see, you'll have to take my advice. It really is the only course, if you want to help Matthew,' Lucille was saying.

'Pardon ... help Matthew? I'm sorry, I didn't quite catch what you said.'

'Matthew's whole life is wrapped up in film-making. Take it away from him and he would be a broken man. It would shatter him absolutely.'

'I don't believe that,' said Joanna with some spirit. 'I can't imagine Matthew a broken man. He's far too tough and strong. I don't know what you're talking about.'

'How do you think Matthew started? Talent isn't enough in the film industry. You need money, and Matthew didn't have any. Oh yes, he had a reputation and a string of awards, but no money. He'd ploughed anything he earned into the next project. That was before my husband came along. He recognised the potential of Matthew's genius and the power of unlimited capital. The result was *Planet Eleven*, which made *Star Wars* look like a video game.'

'I liked *Star Wars*,' said Joanna.

'Matthew went on from where *Star Wars* left off. It was a burst of imagination that was pure genius. But it took money, and my husband was one of the major backers.'

'Your ex-husband...'

'Right, my ex-husband. When we split, I didn't take alimony. I always think alimony is humiliating; it's like being paid for services rendered. Instead I settled for the holding in Matthew's film company. That suited me very nicely.'

So Lucille owned a big chunk of Matthew's assets. Quite a shrewd move. 'Does Matthew know?' Joanna asked.

'No, the transfer did not cause a flutter. I'm sure Matthew has never bothered to see if his backers have changed. I still use the same name. Why should it concern him?'

'Why are you telling me all this?' Joanna's voice was low. She already had an inkling of Lucille's proposal. A thin chill began to evaporate the elation she had felt earlier. This was another, more sophisticated kind of cruelty.

'If I pull out my holding, then Matthew is finished. He'd be bust in a matter of weeks. He employs quite a number of people back in the States. Running any industry these days is expensive. I might want to put my money into something else, something a little more secure.'

Lucille emphasised the last word

fractionally. She meant the security of Matthew's personal attention and company; she wanted no competition. She meant to make sure that there wasn't any.

'But Matthew has plenty of money. He could carry on without you,' said Joanna.

'He wouldn't exactly starve, but he'd have to sack a lot of people. Matthew's a tough man, but he has compassion for people, and he wouldn't like having to see their livelihood disappearing. Nor would he be exactly crazy about the person who caused the break-up, and ruined any prospects of a sequel to *Planet Eleven*.'

'You.'

'No, not me.' Lucille gave a shrill little laugh. 'You, Joanna. If you persist in this ridiculous attachment to Matthew, I swear I'll do it. I'll pull out my stake and Matthew and his precious film company will go straight down the drain. That kind of reality can take the romance out of life.'

Joanna turned away from Lucille, numbed. She could not stand being close to the woman; her perfume was overpowering; her eyes seemed to have narrowed and were lost behind the heavy make-up.

'You wouldn't do it,' said Joanna. 'If you care about Matthew yourself, you couldn't. Destroy somebody like that ... it's inhuman.'

'Oh yes, I care for Matthew. And I'll fight for him. I'll fight every tuppenny-halfpenny female journalist who thinks she fallen for him and that life's going to be a bed of roses from now on.'

'If you think I'm just a gold-digger, out for what I can get, then I won't care enough to be bothered what happens to Matthew,' said Joanna defiantly. 'Your threats won't mean anything.'

'I think you're foolish enough to care very much. You've got that straight, upper-crust English look that even money can't buy. Give him up, Joanna, or I'll ruin his career.'

She broke off as Matthew came out onto the entrance steps, his jacket over his arms. He looked pre-occupied. The luggage was being put into a taxi.

Joanna moved away from Lucille. She could not even bear to speak to her. She said good-bye to Andre.

'I hope you find that young lady,' he said. 'Take care, Joanna. See you at the awards ceremony.'

'Awards ceremony?'

'Everything that Matthew makes wins some kind of prize,' Andre joked. He kissed her cheek in a fatherly salute.

'And this may well be the exception,' said Matthew, grimly. He held the taxi door open for Joanna. 'Get in. We're only just going to make this flight.'

He said a brief good-bye to Lucille, then climbed in beside Joanna, throwing his jacket over the front seat. His face looked dark and set, unapproachable.

'Where are we going?' She almost dared not ask.

'We are flying to Delhi, then catching a connection down to Bombay. We should be there before midnight.'

'Bombay?'

'They apparently took the express train to Delhi, but made inquiries about the air conditioned express from Delhi to Bombay. By flying we'll be there before them.'

'Mandy was not well on the flight over. She doesn't like flying or travel well. I hope she's got the pills I bought her. Look, Matthew,' she tried to sound composed. 'You don't have to come with me. Mandy's my responsibility. I'll find her by myself.'

'Nonsense, you couldn't find a lost elephant by yourself. How could I depend on you? Never. Pierre is a member of my crew and he has no business walking out on a job. Secondly, there's the publicity. If we don't get Mandy back safe and sound, your editor will be down on you like a one-man demolition squad. You'll be out on your ear so fast you won't have time to pick up your street map of London.'

He did not sound like a man who had once said that he loved her, but still the words brought Joanna some crumb of comfort. He cared enough about the situation to be by her

side till they found Mandy. She would think no
further than this drive, sitting next to him,
close in the growing darkness, the warmth of
his body disturbing, then flying through the
night, enclosed in a capsule high above the
Indian plains, sharing, talking, every minute
precious. She was caught in this web of loving
him that was so strong, she could not tear
herself away. Not yet.

As the taxi slowed down to let the rickshaw
boys move out of the way, Joanna caught sight
of the thin ragged boy, Bansi. He was leaning
against his bicycle, half asleep, and leaped up
as the taxi's hooter blared out. He looked
startled, round-eyed, his hands quickly moving
up to protect his face.

'Stop,' said Joanna. 'One moment, please.
I've forgotten something.'

She got out of the taxi and hurried across the
road, her hand fumbling with the clasp of her
handbag. She could not just leave the boy.
That movement, as if he was used to being
struck ...

'I'm going,' she said bluntly. 'This is a
present for you, for your rickshaw. You could
buy a new seat, a bright fringe, a new canopy.
You could make it look really nice.'

She put the roll of rupee notes in his hand.
She had no idea how much she was giving him,
but Bansi was in no doubt. His face broke into
a huge smile.

'Memsahib, I will have the most splendid

rickshaw in Agra! And always for you free rides. You will come back? Yes? Next year?'

'Next year ... perhaps.'

He did not thank her. In his eyes she was rich; she stayed at the Clark's Shiraz; she had enough to eat; she rode in taxis; she came from a rich country across the sea. He was pleased and delighted, but he did not thank her. It was not necessary.

Joanna slipped back into the taxi, her thoughts still with the boy. As she sat back on the leather seat, she felt Matthew's arm come round her. He tipped her face his way, and kissed her with a piercing, stabbing roughness. Then he pushed her away.

'That's why I love you, Joanna,' he said. 'I see you doing something that no one has ever thought of, and then I know why I love you.'

CHAPTER NINE

There was no air conditioning in the old Focke-Friendship, an almost obsolete high-winged plane. It was only a forty-five minute flight, but it was one of the worst flights Joanna had ever experienced. There was nothing romantic about this journey with Matthew as the old plane hit a series of air pockets, lurching, then dropping like a stone.

It flew at an uncomfortable 2,000 feet in a

belt of hot air, the passengers slowly melting in their clumsy aluminium stewpan.

Joanna gazed unhappily out of the tiny window. Matthew seemed to have nerves of steel. He had closed his eyes and was dozing. He had hardly spoken to her.

'Would passengers kindly fasten their seat belts,' came a treacly voice over the tannoy system. 'The pilot apologises for this turbulence. He assures you there is no danger.'

Joanna's fingers were stiff and nerveless, trying to fasten the belt. Matthew leaned across and snapped it into place.

'Sorry about the old plane,' he said eventually. 'I'd have hired a private plane but it couldn't be done at such short notice.'

'I'm beginning to think that the train is the only way to travel in India,' said Joanna, moistening her lips. 'I suppose this is my fault for another ghastly trip.'

'You may be right,' said Matthew. 'But I'm certainly not blaming you for that appalling taxi ride across the plains, and now this. But I did promise I'll make it up to you, and I will. Mandy has a lot to answer for.' His voice was grim.

With overwhelming relief Joanna realised that the plane was losing altitude, and the lights of Delhi were blurred orange glows on the ground.

Suddenly the land rushed towards them as the plane came in to land. Joanna shut her eyes and prayed that the brakes would work. When they finally slowed down, she found she was shaking. She had never been so thankful to get off any plane. She could barely face another flight, but when she realised that the carrier to Bombay was British Airways, her spirits rose. She almost fell onto the big, long haul jumbo in gratitude. Matthew had a word with the hostess and soon as the plane took off, she was at their side with brandies and ice and some hot towels.

The fiery liquid settled Joanna's nerves; before long she slid against Matthew's shoulder and in moments she was asleep, deeply and dreamlessly.

She was still so sleepy at Bombay's Santa Cruz airport that she took in very little of their surroundings. She had to force her eyes open. She left Matthew to retrieve their luggage and get a taxi. It was all noise and bustle and bright lights, and voices clamouring around her. Mandy did indeed have a lot to answer for. So far Joanna had not reckoned the cost of these extra flights; no doubt she would have a struggle to get anything out of the *Daily Post*.

This huge seaport and city was more alive than Delhi and the pace was faster. It was so cosmopolitan and English looking that Joanna felt herself relaxing. Red London buses still lumbered round the city centre even at that time of night.

The taxi drew up outside the Taj Mahal

Inter-Continental Hotel, near Bombay's waterfront. It was one of the most famous hotels in the world; a marriage of Victorian-Saracenic grandeur with a 22-floor modern tower.

The sudden coolness of the vast public rooms came as a shock from the warm night air. Joanna followed Matthew mutely, unable to shake off her lethargy. He had apparently booked a penthouse suite. She did not argue. She did not care where she slept; she would have curled up on the floor.

It was a suite for four people, a family suite and she had a choice of bedrooms. It was beautifully furnished with fine antiques and objets d'art. Joanna had difficulty in believing that she was still in India, till she looked closer at some of the erotic statues, their gods having very earthy pursuits.

'I've ordered a late supper to be sent up,' said Matthew. 'Why don't you change into something loose and comfortable?'

'I don't have anything,' said Joanna.

Matthew returned from his room with his white velvet towelling robe over his arm. He held it out to her. 'You look all right in this,' he said. 'Put it on.'

'Really Matthew, I'm too tired for a seduction scene,' she said. 'I'm almost dead on my feet.'

'You've had nothing since lunch time. A little supper will do you good, then I'll put you to bed with a chaste kiss on your brow. You're quite safe with me.'

He was mocking her again. She felt his eyes on her, scorching her, punishing her with a glance that raked her from head to toe. She stood up, with some dignity, and took the robe.

'Thank you,' she said. 'I'll join you for supper.'

She stood under the shower, naked, letting the tepid water slide over her in a silky waterfall. Her hair clung to her head and neck like a shining burnished helmet. She let it run over her face, splashing on her eyelashes, removing all trace of make-up and the dust of the journey. She was on a dream-like tread-mill. She did not know where it was taking her; she only knew that this would be her last night with Matthew. Tomorrow she would leave him and Lucille would have won. Joanna knew that she loved Matthew so much, she could not harm him in any way.

She had this last one night; a few short hours before the Indian dawn came and the world arrived to claim her attention.

She stepped out of the shower, water still running off her, and wrapped Matthew's white robe round her. She moved towards the other room, her long brown legs glistening, her hair gleaming darkly. The stewards had laid a table with silverware and crystal glasses; a bowl of yellow roses. A trolley held covered dishes. Matthew had dismissed the stewards, saying they would serve themselves.

'Mmn,' sighed Joanna. 'Smells delicious.'

'You smell delicious,' he murmured, taking her swiftly into his arms, his nose buried into the curve of her neck. 'All wet and sweet.'

Joanna struggled against him, pitting her strength, trying to twist herself out of his grip. His arms were like steel.

Joanna felt her body beginning to throb against him, as his lips sought her mouth. His hands deftly moved down to her waist and he untied the belt of the robe, peeling it away from her skin. He held her close, brushing the velvety softness of her back with his palms and fingertips. Her body was melting, tingling, a fire growing within her as his mouth opened hers and their sweet juices merged into a kiss that swept all sane thoughts away.

'I thought you were ... angry with me,' said Joanna, weakly.

'I am.' His voice was low and deep, somewhere in her hair. She was responding with a passion that reached his.

'Matthew, Matthew ...' she cried, clinging to him. She could repeat his name over and over again without giving herself away.

'Gorgeous woman,' he said. 'You've been driving me wild. Darling, darling creature ... don't say no to me now ...'

He lifted her up in his arms and Joanna felt that she was drowning. His eyes were very dark as he carried her through to her white bedroom. He turned off the lights with his elbow and carried her across to the big bed, pulling the cover off before lowering her gently into the pillows. Her skin was gleaming pale and dusky in the light from the window, her hair thrown across the pillows like silk. She held out her arms to him, loving him, wanting him, thinking of nothing but this coming joy. He was so strong and passionate, and yet he was so tender and caring. Where had the arrogant, mocking man gone? This was a gentle giant who crushed her in his arms, his body steely smooth against her, blinding her face with his hair. A kaleidoscope of lights and colours passed across her eyes, like motes of dust ... he was kissing her, a long long kiss that was draining every last vestige of strength from her limbs ...

She was in a pool of childhood memories, floating among half forgotten thoughts. She was sweating, her mouth parched. A fear burrowed through the woolliness in her head, a fear of being ill in a foreign country. It was magnified with isolated thoughts of typhoid and cholera, and Joanna turned this way and that, her thoughts wandering down airy paths of nothingness.

She vaguely heard movements in the bathroom and then her face was being gently washed with a damp cloth. She moved her face so that the dampness would touch her neck.

'Matthew ...?' she murmured.

'I am here,' he answered.

Her eyes were weighted with lead. A strong arm lifted her and a cup was put to her lips.

'Drink this,' he said. 'It'll help.'

'Matthew ... what happened?'

'You passed out on me. I've never known my love-making to have that effect before,' he chuckled mildly. 'Hardly flattering to my male ego.'

'Oh, I'm so sorry ...'

'Dear heart, I should have known you were ill. I'm as tough as old boots, and I'm never ill myself. So it doesn't occur to me that someone else could be more fragile. There, you're looking better now. Your colour is coming back. Sleep, my darling ... you'll be all right by the morning.'

'Don't leave me,' said Joanna, urgently. 'Please don't leave me. Stay here. I'm frightened.'

'No ... never, never ... hush now,' he whispered, stroking her brow, as she slipped back into sleep. She woke, momentarily, to find the room streaked with early morning light. Matthew was stretched out beside her, gently breathing, an arm flung across the space between them. She put a small kiss into his upturned palm and lay back, her fingers touching his. When she awoke again, he had gone.

Joanna grieved because he had gone. It would be like this always now, longing for him

188

and aching for him until the pain died away. She had decided that she would leave him without a word; she would not tell him why.

Joanna dreamed that she was walking in the gardens of the Taj Mahal, hand in hand with Matthew. A mist was rising from the ground and their feet were lost to sight. Somewhere there was a tinkling of bells and a stirring in the ground and Joanna knew that her hundred elephants were restless.

Then the Taj dissolved before their eyes like a reflection in a pool of water disturbed by a stone. There were workmen labouring in the heat in shabby loin-cloths and with rags tied round their heads. Buffalo carts came laden with marble. The air was full of hammering and choking dust.

A tall man stood apart, a great jewel gleaming on his chest. He was watching the army of craftsmen toiling, his face set in a sad sternness. He rolled and unrolled a parchment in his hands, the jewels winking on his brown fingers.

Joanna knew that she was looking at the great Moghul emperor, Shah Jahan, alone and unapproachable. He turned and looked straight at her. His face wore the proud carved features of the Moghul race, but the dark, brooding eyes belonged to Matthew.

She awoke to the sun streaming in through the windows. She felt weak, but the sickness had passed. Someone had put her into a pale pink nightie and her wrist had been rebandaged. There was a knock at her door and a steward came in with tea, passion fruit juice, freshly baked rolls and honey.

She lay back on the pillows, sipping the hot tea, feeling as if she had just surfaced from a sweetly familiar dream.

Her last moments with Matthew had been beautiful; at least she had them to remember.

There was another knock and Matthew came in, handsome in dark blue shirt and slacks, his arms full of flowers ... marigolds, roses, orchids and long stemmed tiger lilies, bought at random in the street market and heaped in profusion.

'An apology,' he said.

'What for?' She kept her eyes on the flowers. 'For being so rude to me yesterday, or for your untimely advances last night?'

'Both,' said Matthew, sitting on the edge of the bed. 'I curse myself for not realising that you were unwell. I couldn't think of anything but making love to you. That's the effect you have on me. Yes, I was angry with you. I still am, but once you were in my arms, all wet and glistening ... it was hopeless.'

'Are you really still annoyed with me?'

'Definitely. Well, perhaps one degree less.'

Joanna fought down her despair. She could go if he was still angry with her, but how hard it would be if he became, once again, the tender lover.

'Feeling well enough to take a surprise?' he went on.

He moved closer to her and tipped up her chin. Their eyes met. They saw the love mixed with doubt, the longings, the passion.

'A surprise?'

'A somewhat chastened Magic Carpet girl, fresh off the train, and alone. I should be prepared for quite a lot of tears. She hasn't stopped crying since the station.'

'Alone?' Joanna was shocked and relieved at the same time. 'But I thought Pierre was with her. Whatever happened?'

'Apparently he discovered some urgent business in Udaipur, such as his career. He put her on the train to Bombay and promised to join her at the week-end. It seemed my wrath was stronger than the attractions of Miss Mandy and he had second thoughts.'

'The poor child...' said Joanna, struggling to get up out of the mass of flowers. 'How absolutely irresponsible of him.'

Matthew pushed her back. 'Stay still, she's here. Come in, Mandy!'

Mandy was indeed chastened. Her face was streaked with tears and the magenta dye had run down the side of her cheeks. She looked a wreck. When she saw Joanna in bed, she burst into fresh tears and flung herself by the side of the bed.

'Oh Joanna, I didn't mean to make you ill! I'm so sorry, I really am,' she sobbed into the

191

sheet.

Joanna ruffled the crimson curls. 'Don't be silly,' she said. 'You didn't make me ill. Worried yes, but not ill. I've only picked up some Indian bug. I'm nearly better anyway.'

'Do you mean it? Really mean it?' Mandy implored her, her clown's face distorted and shining with perspiration. 'I wouldn't have made you ill for worlds.'

'I thought I was a dragon,' Joanna teased. 'Why this sudden change of heart? I should have thought you'd be only too delighted to have me out of the way and unable to boss you about.'

'I'm always saying things I don't really mean,' said Mandy, helping herself to one of Joanna's tissues. 'I don't know why I do it. Anyway, you were bossy—at first. Then you sort of mellowed.'

'A mellow dragon,' commented Matthew from the window. 'Joanna may have become all sweetness and light, but I'm as mad as a hatter at you. Do you realise that you have made mincemeat out of my filming schedule? That Joanna and I travelled most of the night to catch up with you, including a very alarming flight? We're now miles from where we should be, and Joanna is certainly not well enough to travel to Udaipur yet. I have to be back in the States by the end of the week, and I can't see that happening the way things are going.'

'I'm terribly sorry,' said Mandy meekly.

'What did you think you were doing?' asked Joanna, sliding down into the bed. It was years since she had had a day in bed, and she meant to enjoy the luxury. She scooped up an armful of flowers and held them against her face.

'We were eloping,' said Mandy defending herself. She picked up a roll and put butter and honey generously inside it. 'Pierre and I are in love.'

'I'm finding this a little difficult to understand,' said Joanna. 'If you are eloping, why has Pierre left you? Why go to Delhi, if you were coming to Bombay? Why are you in Bombay on your own?'

'Oh Lord, another interrogation,' said Mandy, her mouth full of bread and honey. 'I've told Matthew all this already.'

'Tell me,' said Joanna quietly, but firmly.

Mandy sat herself on the side of the bed, heavily for someone of her small stature. 'We decided to come to Bombay because I was fed up with ruins and temples, and we thought it would be nice to have a few days at the sea-side. I guess you can go straight from Agra to Bombay but I wanted my hair dryer that I left behind at the Ashoka Hotel, and Pierre didn't mind. He's very sweet. They'd kept it for me, wasn't that kind? Then Pierre started worrying about his job, and the film. He didn't want to break his contract with Matthew and he started getting all French, and I could see it was going to be on his mind, just when I wanted to be the only thing on his mind.'

Her tears had dried and she was regaining some of her usual perkiness.

'So he fixed me up a room at the Sun-n-Sands Hotel, which is right on the beach, and said he'd join me at the week-end. I didn't like the idea at first, but I could see the point about his job. After all, if we're going to get married, he can't be out of work.'

'Well, Bombay isn't exactly the sea-side,' was all Joanna could think to say. 'It's a seaport facing the Arabian Sea.'

'It's got a beach, hasn't it?'

'Juhu Beach,' said Joanna. 'But I doubt if it's anything like your idea of an English resort.'

'I don't care,' said Mandy. 'I just want to swim and sunbathe and walk along the sand. The scenery doesn't bother me.'

'Well, you'll have time to do that now,' said Matthew. 'I want you to stay here and look after Joanna till she's better.'

'But what about you?' Joanna knew the answer before she had even asked the question. Matthew had been distancing himself from them all during Mandy's monologue. Her intuition was right. He was back with his mind on his work, the troublesome Mandy having been found and Pierre returned to his rightful course.

'I shall be returning to Udaipur immediately,' said Matthew. 'A doctor is coming up to see you this morning, Joanna, just to make sure you're all right. I can't leave the most romantic city of all India in Lucille's hands. A phantom palace floating on the blue waters of an artificial lake; all those houseboats; pinnacles of amber and jade. She'll murder it.'

'But you left Lucille with instructions to film...'

He gave a quick, half-grin, but without a hint of apology. 'I didn't want her tagging along. She has a disturbing habit of acting as if I'm already husband number four.'

'And aren't you?' asked Mandy, archly.

'No, I'm not.'

'What about Mandy ...?' sighed Joanna, feeling sad and lost again. 'Don't you need her for your filming? It is supposed to be about her trip.' Already events were taking Matthew away from her.

'No, she's going to stay here and take care of you. I don't want anything to go wrong. She can phone me anytime.'

'Please, it isn't necessary,' Joanna protested. 'I'm feeling so much better. Take Mandy back with you, and leave me here to sleep. That's all I want to do ... sleep and sleep. She'll just be wasting her time here. Take her with you ... the filming really is more important. Matthew, finish your work with Mandy.'

Her voice fell away, a faint shine of perspiration on her brow. She was tired now. The arrival of Mandy, first sobbing but now exuberant, had wearied her. Perhaps she had been more ill than she thought.

'You could hire a nurse for Joanna,' Mandy suggested, torn between seeing Pierre again and sunbathing by the sea.

'Yes, a nurse,' said Joanna drowsily.

When she awoke again, they had gone. The flowers had been cleared from her bed and were in vases all round the room. The bed was smooth and neatly made around her, and a thermometer stood in a glass of water, a clinical touch. A woman was sitting in the doorway, her white uniform immaculate, her ankles neatly crossed. She was reading a magazine. As Joanna stirred, the woman looked up and smiled reassuringly.

'Hello...' began Joanna and went back to sleep again.

It was evening before she eventually surfaced. She felt refreshed and hungry. She sat up in bed and the nurse came over to her.

'Namaste, Miss Hamilton,' she said, her hands joined together in traditional greeting. 'I hope you are feeling better. You have slept well.'

'I'm hungry!'

'That's a good sign. I will order a light supper for you.'

Joanna nodded her thanks and turned her head. On the table beside the bed was the tiny amber elephant from the Amber Palace. There was no need for a note or words. The little elephant said it all; she had never felt more close to Matthew even though they were already miles apart.

The steward brought a standing tray for her bed with a fragrant chicken soup and a light, fluffy omelet. She ate soberly but with a growing appetite. She had to regain her strength quickly; a lingering convalescence was no part of her plans.

The next morning Joanna telephoned the Lake Palace Hotel at Udaipur but they were all out, taking advantage of the morning coolness and light. In a way she was glad that she had spoken to no one. It made what she had to do that much easier.

In the afternoon she took a tourist launch across Bombay harbour to Elephanta Island. High-prowed fishing boats headed towards the open sea, passing tankers now riding light having unloaded their oil at the refineries on Butcher Island. Modern ocean liners on luxury cruises nosed their way through the mass of smaller craft in the harbour, sunlight glinting on the cabin windows.

She did not want to leave Bombay without seeing the cave temples and huge sculptures. But she was still weak and the excursion tired her. She stood in front of the eighteen foot triple image of the Hindu Trinity: Brahma, Siva and Vishnu, her gaze mesmerised by their stern and loving faces.

As Joanna lingered, she found the darkness

soothing, like a calm hand on her forehead.

She came out into the light and stood away from the crowds to look across to the harbour and city. She was standing between the two great eternities, the vast past and the teeming future. The only thing she could be sure of was today.

As the plane lifted off from Santa Cruz airport that evening, she looked down on the twinkling lights of Bombay and felt a great sadness. She doubted if she would ever see India again. It had been a once-in-a-lifetime glimpse of a magical country. Nor would she ever see Matthew again. She would have to learn how to forget him.

CHAPTER TEN

Fleet Street was wind-swept and wet; the red London Transport buses and beetle-black taxis crawled along the narrow street in its usual traffic hold-up leading to Ludgate Circus and the hill to St Paul's Cathedral. Overhead a helicopter wheeled over towards the Thames, taking shots for some news programme.

Joanna lowered her head against the depressing combination of damp and cold; the rain was fickle, falling in a drizzle that was not quite enough for an umbrella but still succeeded in making everyone and everything uncomfortably damp. She had been back from India a week; off sick for most of that time with the virus she had picked up there.

But now she had recovered enough to return to work, and this morning she was to see Mr Wilberforce in his office. She knew she was due for a reprimand; she was prepared for the worst. He had not been overjoyed to find that she had left Mandy behind in India, even with illness as an excuse.

It was always strange returning to work after a holiday or sickness, but this time Joanna found it even more difficult to revert to her old routine. Matthew was constantly in her thoughts.

Her desk had been invaded by the other reporters in editorial and was piled with newspapers, cuttings and old coffee cups.

'How nice,' said Joanna, tipping the rubbish off her typewriter. 'Naturally I do want to read every single word you all wrote while I was away, but not right now.'

'So how was India, Joanna?'

'Fabulous. I'd go back tomorrow.'

'I hear you lost the Magic Carpet girl.'

'That's right. Word got back that you were short of front page news, so I made the ultimate sacrifice. I shall expect a generous whip-round for a leaving present.'

'He's mad at you all right, but not that mad.'

Joanna had lost weight over the last week, and her cheeks had a fine, delicate hollowness.

Although she had deliberately closed her mind to thoughts of Matthew, still his presence haunted her. She could hear his voice mocking her, laughing at her, then whispering tenderly in her ear.

'Come in, I've been expecting you, Joanna,' said Mr Wilberforce. 'I trust you're fully recovered.'

'Yes, thank you.'

'Sit down. Now, I want a full explanation, young woman.'

Edgar Wilberforce had the thin, ulcer-worn look of a hard working editor. Joanna had always admired him and the efficient way he ran the newspaper.

'I consider that what you did was totally irresponsible,' he went on, before Joanna could even open her mouth. 'Mandy Robbins was a guest of the *Daily Post* and you were supposed to take care of her. If anything has happened to her, Joanna, then you're in big trouble. One thing I insist on is the total reliability of my editorial staff, and I consider that you let the *Daily Post* down.'

Joanna shrank in her chair, waiting for the worst.

'I'm sure she's all right, Mr Wilberforce,' said Joanna. 'She's in good company. The film crew ... and Matthew Howard ... they won't let any harm come to Mandy.'

'You might be sure, but I doubt if Mandy's mother will be overjoyed to hear that you abandoned her daughter in—where was it? Udaipur?'

'Bombay,' Joanna sighed.

'Bombay? What were you doing in Bombay? It wasn't on the itinerary.'

'Er—no. Well, you see, Mandy had an urge for a little break on the coast. The heat, you know, and all those ruins and temples. It can get anyone down, and Mandy really did suffer from the heat.'

'No doubt. All the more reason for you to have kept a closer eye on her. She's due at Heathrow tomorrow morning, and I hope for your sake, Joanna, that she arrives all in one piece. The other newspapers will love it if she has a case against us.'

Joanna kept her face deliberately void of emotion. It all depended on how Mandy had enjoyed the last few days with Pierre. If it had all gone wrong, she was quite likely to return home in a mood, ready to blame anyone, Joanna and the *Daily Post* in particular.

'I'll go and meet her,' Joanna offered.

'You do that,' said Mr Wilberforce curtly. 'And think yourself lucky you've still got a job.'

'Yes, Mr Wilberforce. Did you like Mandy's Diary?'

'I'd have liked it better if you could have completed it. I don't like a series half finished. I'll expect the rest of your copy by six o'clock tomorrow evening.'

Joanna escaped. She realised that she had been let off quite lightly. It must mean that Mr Wilberforce had liked what she had written, and had accepted her illness as the reason for returning early to London. It would have been difficult to get another job on Fleet Street; so many newspapers were cutting their staff.

She did not want to spend the evening alone so she joined some colleagues in a wine bar off Fleet Street. She sat in the smoke laden atmosphere, cradling a glass of chilled dry white wine which gradually warmed up from the steamy atmosphere of the bar. Her clothes were still damp and she knew she should get home soon to dry off. A hot bath would be bliss and perhaps the late night old film on television.

But the flat would be empty and if she was not careful then her thoughts would fly back to India and Matthew. Perhaps he was already on his way to the States.

She gave up trying to work it out. Matthew was somewhere, no doubt with Lucille, with the mammoth task of cutting and editing his film ahead of him; his genius and inspiration would take those very ordinary scenes of Mandy and the wonders of India and turn them into magic. No doubt she would get a chance to see the film …

Her heart turned over and she almost spilled her drink as her hand slipped. If she saw a preview of the documentary, then she might see Matthew . . . a surge of pain constricted her breathing for a moment. It would be unbearable.

'I must go,' she said, standing up. 'Thanks for the drink.' She put it down on the table, untouched. ''Night everyone.'

''Night Joanna. Take care. Don't overdo it. No all night parties.'

She smiled wanly. 'I'll remember your advice.'

She walked down the poorly lit street; the great printing machines were spilling out copies of morning newspapers; office lights were on where subs still worked on the front page of the next edition.

If she closed her eyes she could almost imagine Matthew by her side, so tall and strong, so protective. His hand in hers would be comforting like a rock but not a chain. He would have respected her independence, allowed her to grow as a person and develop her identity. However much he had tried to impose his will, he had never once tried to destroy her spirit.

How much she loved everything about him, even his maddening arrogance. She understood him, accepted him and if she had had time fully to know him, it would have been an intimate relationship with worth above all others. They would have walked on a plane of their own, knowing each other so well that the quality of every simple activity would have been enhanced beyond belief.

She tipped an expensive Tweed bath oil into her bath and soaked in the hot water till she almost fell asleep from the warmth. At least her small flat was warm and welcoming, furnished with old pieces of furniture that she had bought with care and restored with patience, and other much loved pieces from her old home. These familiar things were all a comfort now. She had put the amber elephant on the shelf among her tiny ornaments. She thought of the great lumbering creature she had seen on the road to Agra, lifting logs in its trunk to load onto a lorry, its long uncertain life one of labour for mankind.

Outside the rain had turned into a steady downpour, splattering the windowpanes with the drumming of wet fingertips. Joanna lay in bed listening to the sound, wondering about the empty years that stretched ahead like a desert; would she always be alone like this, with no hand to touch or warm body close by her?

She could work and there was solace in that. The notes she had brought from India were burning a hole in a file, demanding to be written up into some coherent form. She did not want to write a feature about India ... it had been done so many times and she was not a travel writer. A story perhaps ... something about the Lady of the Taj ...

She fell asleep, tears unshed but they were there all the same, and she cried in her sleep unaware that her cheeks were wet until she awoke suddenly as if from a bad dream.

She sat up in the darkened room, afraid, clutching the sheet to her. It had been a very bad dream. Only it was no dream. She had lost Matthew. She would wake again in the morning and the pain would still be there.

First thing before breakfast Joanna checked on the arrival time of the flight from Delhi. It was, according to the latest information, going to be an hour late because of head winds. She decided she would have time to go into the office and look keen, before taking the underground train to Heathrow. She was going to have to work very hard to restore Mr Wilberforce's confidence in her.

She wore her newest outfit, a collarless jacket and long full skirt in a soft blend of brown and cobalt blue wool. A leather bound waistcoat added extra warmth. Her boots were a supple caramel suede, laced at the side. She scooped her hair up onto the top of her head and secured it with her mother's pins. The result was stunning and the admiring glances as she travelled to work were a boost to her morale.

She was glad to find she had a busy day ahead. The chief reporter had put her down in the diary for a variety of stories, from a tower block protest by tenants to a beauty contest at the Lyceum in the evening.

'Say, don't you fellows want this Miss UK

ticket?' she asked, waving the piece of cardboard around. 'All those high-cut swimsuits and leggy ladies.'

'If the judges have any sense they'll award the crown to you. Hey, tell us what happened in India! You look quite different.'

Her face softened, then saddened and she turned away quickly, pretending to look out of the smoked window, down into Fleet Street.

'It was the heat and all that curry,' she said lightly. 'Curry definitely does something to the complexion.'

They laughed and Joanna had survived the moment.

She applied herself to writing an instalment of Mandy's Diary. The final episode would have to wait until she met Mandy, and could have a talk with her.

Joanna caught sight of the clock. She was cutting it fine. She picked up her bag and hurried down the stairs, not waiting for the lift. She went through the swing doors into the street and straight into a man who had just got out of a taxi.

She gasped and moved back, but his hands were gripping her arms. She looked up, startled.

'Joanna. Joanna, darling ... at last.'

She was in his arms, clinging to him, not caring about the jostling pedestrians, the amused glances. She was laughing, half crying, oblivious to anything but the joy of seeing

Matthew again. His dear face was a mixture of worry and relief; that deep short laugh that she loved so much coming between his words.

'Don't ever leave me again ... Joanna darling, I've been through hell.'

His mouth swooped down on her lips. Fleet Street loved it. People stared from buses. A messenger boy almost fell off his bicycle. Typists hurrying to lunch passed by with smiles on their faces.

How could his lips be soft, and yet hard and demanding at the same time? The kiss seemed like eternity to Joanna: she never wanted it to end; but they broke away, smiling at each other, trembling a little.

'Matthew, it's really you ...'

'I hope you're not kissing a stranger,' he teased. 'Not like that ... it could get you into trouble.'

'Oh Matthew, I never expected to see you again.'

'Foolish girl. When are you going to believe me? I love you and I mean it.'

'And I love you. Matthew darling, I love you so much,' her voice was faltering, but her eyes were glowing. If he could read her eyes, then he need look no further. He flung his arm round her shoulders, a gesture that was so particularly his, and began to walk her away from the newspapers' offices. His stride was buoyant, his fingers gripping her flesh as if to make sure that she was real. They saw no one;

the hurrying crowds were no more than ghosts passing by. There was only each other.

'But why are you here?' she asked, quickening her step to keep up with him. 'You're supposed to be in the States.'

'I came after you,' he said sternly. 'A fine dance you've led me. You're worse than Mandy, and she's only a child. I couldn't take the risk of you marrying Mr Wilberforce on the rebound. I've flown half way across the world in pretty much the wrong direction, just to see you.'

'But why me? Why me?' she asked, still incredulous.

He turned her to face a shop window. It was a book shop and the customers turned to look at Joanna. The assistant looked up and followed their gaze. Joanna saw herself reflected in the window.

'Look at yourself,' said Matthew. 'Joanna Hamilton, you are a raving beauty ... look at that face, that hair, that smile hovering in those gorgeous eyes. Look at that spirit, that determination, that streak of stubbornness ... all the things that make me love you. This time, you're not going to get away, not like Mandy.'

'Mandy!' said Joanna, aghast. 'I've got to go and meet her. Oh, Matthew, I almost forgot.'

'Slow down. She's here. We flew over together. It seemed a sensible arrangement. I thought I'd keep an eye on her for you.'

Joanna let her breath go in a big sigh. 'The

208

things you do for me. Thank you. I'm already in enough hot water. But I thought your flight was going to be late.'

'We made up the time and arrived on schedule. But don't worry about Mandy. She was met by her mother and a string of boyfriends. She has quite a fan club. I imagine she'll have forgotten about Pierre in a fortnight.'

'I shall have to go and see her as I've the Diary to finish,' said Joanna. 'Matthew, I've got an awful lot of work to do today. My job's on the line, and I'm really lucky to get a second chance.'

'I kept some notes for you. Some of Mandy's prize remarks. I don't like to see anything unfinished.'

'You never cease to amaze me,' said Joanna. 'To even think of it. Thank you. I was worried in case I couldn't do it, without being there. What happened during those last few days with Pierre? Were they still planning a future together?'

'No. Strangely enough, their little romance seemed to evaporate on the shores of Lake Pichola. They were still friendly, very friendly, but it was as if their sudden elopement to Delhi was the moment when they went over the top, and from then onwards it was all downhill. Pierre became very serious about his work and produced some marvellous sounds in Udaipur. Mandy, too, began to wonder about her future, and we had plenty of time to talk about it on the flight home.'

Joanna smiled and nodded. 'I'm not surprised. I couldn't ever see it working ... Mandy's head was full of dreams of being in one of your films, or becoming a television personality.'

'We had a long talk about the film industry. Eventually Mandy decided that she really wasn't cut out for all those early dawn starts, hanging about for hours, retaking shots a dozen times, learning lines. What she really is interested in is make-up. So, next term, she's going to enrol for a beauty and make-up course in London, with a view to joining the make-up department of a television studio.'

'And you're paying for it?' Joanna guessed.

'I never said I was.'

'I know you, now.'

'Tell Mr Wilberforce you want the day off. I've got a lot I want you to do,' he remarked, changing the subject. 'Call him up from that phone box.'

Joanna stopped in the middle of the narrow pavement. Surely they were not going to fight now about her job, and her need to work? She thought she had made that clear.

'My job is already shaky,' she said. 'I'm not going to prejudice my position in any way. If you had some filming to do, you'd go and do it, wouldn't you? Darling, I want to be with you just as much as you, believe me, but we are going to have to wait—at least until this evening.'

'What about lunch? Does Mr Wilberforce allow you to eat?' Matthew had a dangerous glint in his eyes. He looked as if he might march into the editor's office and demand Joanna's release.

'Of course,' she said with a laugh. 'As long as I don't take too long.'

'I can see I am going to have to be patient, but not for long. Darling Joanna, let's get married as soon as possible. How long does it take to get a special licence? I telephoned the agents for the Barbican and they have a penthouse flat available in a month's time. You could walk to work. Save on fares. Then when we're settled we could start looking round for a week-end home ... the Cotswolds, Devon, Dorset ... anywhere you like, perhaps something old and rambling? What do you think?'

'Don't rush me,' Joanna implored. 'A penthouse flat, the Barbican, the Cotswolds ... please, Matthew, you're going too fast. I haven't said anything about marrying you.'

'We'll need two cars, of course,' Matthew went on. 'I expect you'd prefer a Mini, whatever I buy for myself,' he added mockingly. 'I warn you that it'll probably be another Rolls.'

'I thought you lived in Los Angeles,' said Joanna helplessly. 'Your work is there and your home. I don't understand.'

'I'm coming back to England, if that's where you want to be,' said Matthew, his expression serious. 'My next film will be on location in Spain, so my time in the States would be minimal. And the sequel to *Planet Eleven*— well, that could be filmed anywhere in the world—India perhaps.'

His words made Joanna catch her breath; then she remembered Lucille and her threat. Joanna had forgotten it in the joy of seeing Matthew again, when she had thought he had gone from her life forever. Now it grew like a spectre, dark and menacing.

'Matthew, I can't marry you,' she blurted out. 'Because of Lucille.'

'Lucille? What's Lucille got to do with us? She's gone back to the States. What do you mean?'

He took her arm and began to walk her purposefully towards the Aldwych and the Strand. He was wearing a dark grey suit; and Joanna suddenly realised it was the first time she had seen him in a suit. He wore no overcoat or waistcoat and he looked like a business executive, not a brilliantly inventive film maker.

'Matthew, if I marry you, then you'll go broke . . . bankrupt. There won't be any filming in Spain, no sequel to *Planet Eleven*. Lucille will make sure that you don't.'

'I don't understand a word of this,' he said

grimly. 'But do go on.'

'Her ex-husband was your principal backer, wasn't he? Well, when they divorced Lucille took over his holdings in your company instead of alimony. You probably never even knew. If I . . . if we hadn't . . .' She did not know how to go on. There was a tight feeling across her breast and her breath quivered. 'Matthew, if we get married, Lucille will pull out her stake. Your company will collapse, and you'd be ruined. You'd have to start all over again.'

'Is that why you left me, running away from Bombay as soon as my back was turned?' He touched her elbow, an action both gentle and electrifying. 'Tell me the truth.'

'Yes, that's why,' she sighed. 'I happen to think your work is important. I couldn't be the cause of all those wonderful ideas withering. I know that your sequel to *Planet Eleven* is going to be a huge success, and a milestone in cinema history.'

'You little goose,' said Matthew, a new warmth in his dark eyes. 'All this sacrifice for me. Lucille knew just how to handle your emotions, didn't she? My darling, I am very very touched and moved, but I think we can call Lucille's bluff on two counts.'

He tucked her arm a little closer to him. 'Firstly, the profits from *Planet Eleven* are still pouring in, and although I need millions of dollars to back any new project, I'll never be exactly on the bread line. I could always do something else ... work for another film studio; make television commercials,' he joked.

'Matthew, that's not funny.'

'But the main point is that although I may not have been aware of my change of backer; nor did my accountants inform me; I'm afraid Lucille has overlooked something. She obviously did not read the small print. When I set up my company, I wanted to make sure the money would be there, however long it might take me to make *Planet Eleven*. I didn't want my backers getting cold feet half way through the filming and leaving me with an unfinished epic on my hands. A special clause was inserted, and certainly Lucille's husband knew about this. It stipulates that the money cannot be withdrawn for ten years under any circumstances. And that was four years ago, Joanna. So there are still six years to run, and who cares what happens in six years' time? You and I are going to make our own future. We'll be travelling the world, making films; or bringing up an enormous family in an old Victorian house on Richmond Hill; or publishing a weekly newspaper somewhere in Cornwall, you as the editor and me doing the art work.'

Joanna's expression was calm but her heart was racing. She had suffered so much since Lucille's threat, it did not seem possible that there could be such a simple means of removing it.

'She can't do this then,' said Joanna. 'Your company is quite safe?'

'You can stop worrying about it. You and I are getting married right away. We've six glorious years ahead before I have to join the dole queue. We'd better make the most of it, darling girl. Do you fancy a champagne celebration lunch at the Savoy, or a cup of instant coffee at your flat?'

Joanna's heart almost turned over as Matthew stood there, looking down at her, his eyes devouring her as if he had never seen a woman before. There was a moment of waiting, each hardly daring to believe that they really loved each other; that they had found a partner for a lifetime.

'I make very good coffee,' said Joanna softly.

Matthew stepped sideways to the edge of the pavement and flagged down a passing taxi.

'And I can't resist good coffee,' he said, opening the door.

Far away in India, the constant stream of pilgrims walked along the peaceful gardens towards the shining white shrine to married love. The heat of the scorching sun cradled the land in a shimmering haze, bathing the Taj in light.

And Joanna's hundred ivory elephants stirred and shifted more deeply into the dry earth.